SEALS

Before he had a chance to move, the firing broke out. No longer was it ten, twelve men shooting at one another. Now there were fifty or sixty of them. He could hear them shouting in Vietnamese. It was too late to get out. The open ground behind him, the rice paddy, would become a killing ground if he tried to escape. Around him, he could hear the firefight. Weapons on full auto. Grenades, shouts, cries, and groans. The sound rose and fell like the surf hitting a beach.

It was all over, he was sure. He'd led his men into an ambush. There was no escape...

STRONGHOLD

SEALS
STRONGHOLD

STEVE MACKENZIE

AVON BOOKS  NEW YORK

AVON BOOKS
A division of
The Hearst Corporation
105 Madison Avenue
New York, New York 10016

First Avon Books Printing: March 1989

AVON TRADEMARK REG. U.S. PAT. OFF. AND IN OTHER COUNTRIES, MARCA REGISTRADA, HECHO EN U.S.A.

Printed in the U.S.A.

K–R   10   9   8   7   6   5   4   3   2   1

1

Sergeant David Sinclair glanced to the right where the first squad crouched, then waved a hand, signaling them forward. Together they swept out of the tree line and into the rice paddies that bordered the small hamlet. Part of the hamlet was protected by a finger of jungle that reached down and shaded it from the brutal tropical sun, embracing the mud and thatch hootches that looked as if a strong wind or heavy rain could wash them away. A few people—old men with long white beards, women in black pajama bottoms and raw silk shirts—sat in the little shade of the hootches as nude children ran around them. A water buffalo bellowed from its pen on one side of a dilapidated hootch, but no one paid attention to it.

Sinclair stopped momentarily on the top of a rice paddy dike. He wiped the sweat from his face with the sleeve of his faded jungle fatigues, shifted his M16 to his right hand, the butt against his hip, and stared out across the paddy and into the village, like the great white hunter on the plains of the African veldt.

Keeping his eyes on the hamlet, he stepped into the tepid water that poured over the top of his boot, filling it with the sewage-laden water. He didn't notice it. The water was too warm to cool his tired feet. Too warm, and too filthy for relief.

The whole platoon was out of the trees now, moving toward the village. No one there paid them the slightest attention. All villagers in South Vietnam had learned long ago that it was best to ignore the armed strangers; let them do what they wanted and they would soon leave.

Sinclair was moving through the foul-smelling water, stepping on the rice plants to keep his foot from sinking deep into the mud. Again he glanced right and left, squinting in the glare of the sun reflecting from the water. The stench from the paddy assaulted him, so he breathed through his mouth, trying not to smell it. Sweat soaked him, turning his fatigues black down the back, under the arms, and around the waist.

As he reached a dike fifty yards from the edge of the village, the people suddenly seemed to spot them. One old man looked up, startled, and shouted something in high-pitched Vietnamese. Two women dropped the sticks they were using to stir a bubbling pot and fled. Another grabbed one of the little girls and ran for the jungle behind them.

Sinclair didn't wait to see more. He dived forward, splashing into the water as he ducked his head and snapped the safety on his M16 to single shot.

"Take cover!" he roared when he saw his men standing. "Take cover, fuck heads!"

Sinclair turned his attention back to the village that was now deserted except for the water buffalo roaring and straining at the rope tied to the ring in its nose.

For an instant, Sinclair had time to examine the scene that was suddenly vacant and quiet: a single cook fire still burning, the light woodsmoke lost in the blaze of the hot afternoon sun; and no movement in the village now that the people had disappeared.

The lieutenant, a young man so fresh to Vietnam that his fatigues were still bright green and the butter bar on his collar seemed to glow with a radiance that demanded he be one of the first targets, dropped into the water next to Sinclair. Filth from the paddy splashed up onto Sinclair.

"Christ, sir, take it easy."

The lieutenant ducked his head once as an apology and mumbled, "Sorry."

Sinclair wiped his face in the crook of his elbow and then slid down so that the top of his helmet was no longer visible from the village. He was lying nearly prone, the water covering most of his body, soaking his equipment and ammunition. He stared up into the bright blue cloudless sky and waited for all hell to break loose.

"What's happening?" the lieutenant asked.

"Ambush," said Sinclair.

The lieutenant rolled to his stomach and raised up, peeking over the top of the dike. He stared into the deserted village and then dropped down again. "How do you know?"

Sinclair shook his head and wondered where all the kids came from, not realizing that Lieutenant Boyson was two years older than he was. It was the inexperience that concerned Sinclair. The lieutenant wouldn't last another week if he didn't straighten out.

"When the villagers run, there is an ambush nearby. You can count on it."

"Maybe they're afraid of us," responded the lieutenant.

"No sir, they got out. Something's going to happen soon."

To the left, one man stood up and then took a single step forward. He stopped again, unsure of what to do.

The machine gun opened fire then. The bullets stitched across the water, splashing their way toward the man. He dived to the right and rolled into the shadow of the dike. Several rounds slammed into the mud with dull, wet slaps.

"Open fire!" screamed the lieutenant. "Open fire!"

Around them was the rattling of the M16 as the men began to fire into the village. The M60 began to hammer, the rounds walking across the walls of a mud hootch and then to the remains of a broken-down oxcart. The grenadier rolled to his left, aimed, and fired a single round at the hamlet. It fell short, exploding into a tiny cloud of red dust and black smoke.

Sinclair put a hand to the side of his mouth and ordered, "Cease fire. Cease fire."

"Why?" asked the lieutenant.

"Because we're no longer taking incoming."

"How can you tell?"

"Christ, sir, listen. We're hearing 16s and an M60, but nothing from the enemy."

Again the lieutenant risked a look into the village and again he saw nothing there except for the water buffalo, now lying on its side, bleeding, and a haze of dirt stirred up by the machine and rifle fire.

"So what do we do?"

Sinclair shrugged but said, "The smart thing would

be to call in artillery, level the place, and then sweep the smoking ruins."

"We can't just shell an innocent village."

Sinclair stared into the baby face of the officer. "Innocent village? They shot at us."

"Yeah, well," said Boyson.

Sinclair rolled over and crawled up the dike so that he could peek over the top of it. Fifty yards of open ground separated him from the edge of the village. A second dike about twenty-five meters away would provide some cover, but there was an awful lot of open ground. He had no idea where the enemy gunner was hiding if he was still in the village.

"Artillery's out?" asked Sinclair.

"We saw innocent women and children in that village," said the lieutenant.

"Yes sir, but they did nothing to warn us about the VC."

"They ran off," said the lieutenant. "That clued you quick enough."

Sinclair nodded, knowing that it wasn't time to argue about the innocence or guilt of the people in the village. They had to do something to get out of the paddy without getting a bunch of his people killed.

To the right was another finger of jungle. One of the dikes provided cover to it. Now, if the enemy was clever, he would have a second ambush set there, waiting for the Americans to observe that they could escape in that direction. Sinclair grinned to himself and then glanced up toward the sun. It was midafternoon with five, six hours of light left. Plenty of time to extract himself from the rice paddy without getting any of his men killed by hurrying to please the lieutenant, who didn't know what the hell he was doing.

Without a word to the lieutenant, Sinclair crawled

to the right, his head down, his nose nearly in the dirty water. He ignored the odor, as he reached the radio operator. The man lay on his stomach in the corner of the paddy, trying to keep the radio dry without exposing himself to enemy gunfire. He gripped the antenna in one hand, holding it down so that the VC wouldn't be able to see it.

As he got close, Sinclair snapped his fingers and held out his hand, waiting for the handset. He took it and said, "Get me arty advisory."

The RTO flipped the pre-sets, and the radio cycled through the frequencies with an audible squeal. When it stopped, Sinclair raised the telephonelike handset to his head and said, "Arty advisory, arty advisory, this is Red Rider one five with a fire mission over."

"Red Rider one five, this is Duc Lap arty. Go."

Sinclair tried to remember the procedure that he had learned in basic training so long ago. The old lieutenant had taken care of the procedure for the last few months.

"Duc Lap arty, I have a fire mission, over."

"Roger, fire mission."

Sinclair realized that he needed the coordinates from a map. He remembered, basically, where the village was, but close didn't count. He needed the exact coordinates. He handed his rifle to the RTO and pulled his map from his pocket. Water had soaked through the plastic to eat at the paper, but he could still make out the grids. He studied it for a moment and then fed the coordinates to Duc Lap arty.

"Shot, over" was the only reply.

"Shot, out," said Sinclair, remembering that from listening to the old lieutenant.

A moment later there was a rattling overhead that fell into the rice paddies to the west of the finger of jungle. Sinclair squeezed the handset. "Add one hundred. Left fifty."

"Shot, over."

"Shot, out."

The plume of black-gray smoke that followed a few moments later grew out of the center of the finger of the jungle. Sinclair nodded and said, "On target. Need HE with contact fusing. Fire for effect."

Sinclair gave the handset back to the RTO and then moved around so that he could see better. The onrushing train roared overhead and there was a series of crashing detonations in the trees. Loud crashes as the artillery exploded and then geysers of dirt thrown up into the sky. Shrapnel whined, slamming into the trunks of the trees, ripping at the leaves and the smaller plants.

A second volley of six raced over and detonated, and then a third. The dirt mushroomed skyward, then rained down, and the top of the jungle seemed to be on fire, a dark, brown smoke from the artillery rising above it and drifting away on a light, almost nonexistent breeze.

"Last rounds on the way," said the radio.

The RTO acknowledged the call. Sinclair watched the jungle and when he heard the rounds overhead, he was up and moving. He shouted at the first squad, waving them forward. He ran through the rice paddy in slow motion, pumping his arms and legs, splashing the water. He held his M16, retrieved from the RTO, up away from his body, trying to keep it dry.

He reached one dike, leaped to the top, and then dropped into the water. In front of him, he heard the last of the artillery rounds hit the jungle. The roar from the rounds ripped through the quiet, overpowering it. And then it was silent, except for the sound of the men running through the water. The splashing of the feet and the grunting of effort as the men tried to cover the ground that sucked at them, trying to draw them down.

Sinclair reached the edge of the jungle, a wall of green that rose in front of him like a curtain in a theater. He slipped to a stop and dropped to one knee. With his free hand he reached out to part the veil of vines and branches from lacy ferns. Moisture rolled out at him like he had just opened the door of a steam bath. Sweat bathed his face as he breathed hard, trying to fill his lungs.

Just as the other men reached the jungle, there was a single burst of fire. The bullets from the RPD snapped through the vegetation. One man grunted and fell, blood spreading on his chest.

Now it was too late for artillery because they were too close. Sinclair hesitated, pleased with figuring out the ambush, but disappointed the artillery hadn't done a better job of destroying it.

He flipped his selector switch to full auto and got to his feet. "Let's go," he shouted as he plunged into the jungle.

At first, he could see nothing in the semi-darkness. The greens, browns, and blacks concealed the enemy. The chattering of the machine gun, joined by several AKs, was off to the left. He stopped for a moment, letting his eyes adjust to search for the enemy.

There was movement to the right and Sinclair froze. He waited, saw the khaki of a North Vietnamese regular. Slowly, he raised his weapon and aimed. The enemy soldier moved again and Sinclair could see the side of the man's head. He squeezed the trigger and the weapon fired. There was a splash of red as the man's head exploded and he dropped from sight.

With that, Sinclair was moving again, listening to the sounds of firing around him. No longer was he aware of the heat or the humidity. The cotton that had filled his mouth was gone. The only thing that mattered was the enemy machine gunner firing in an almost steady burst into the rice paddies.

From somewhere one of his men shouted, "Grenade!" Sinclair crouched, keeping his head up. He hadn't heard the grenade fall and figured that the dense vegetation would protect him.

There was a single, muffled blast and the machine gun fell silent. Now there was shouting in Vietnamese. AKs were firing steadily on full auto. The rounds sprayed through the trees and bushes, ripping at the bark, the leaves, the vines. Bits of vegetable matter swirled around. Smoke hung in the air. Cordite was heavy.

Sinclair moved cautiously, his head swinging from side to side as he searched for the enemy. There was a ripping as an M16 opened up, and then more as others fired. Still, Sinclair couldn't find a target. He moved on, deeper into the jungle. Then, through the gaps in the trees, he saw a man in black pajamas moving slowly toward the rear. Sinclair leaned against the trunk of a huge tree and took a bead. When his sights were centered on the man's back, he squeezed the trigger, letting the rifle fire itself. The round took the man in the middle of the back, lifting him forward and then slamming him to the ground. As he fell, he tossed his weapon up into the air.

Firing erupted around him. Sinclair slipped to one knee and listened. There were men running through the jungle near him. There was a flash of movement and he saw an American leap a log before disappearing behind a bush. Bullets ripped through the air where the man had been. Sinclair spotted the muzzle flash and fired on full auto, hosing down the jungle.

When the bolt locked back, he sank to the jungle floor, his back to the tree. He released the empty magazine, pulled out a new one, and saw that the top of it was covered with crud from the rice paddy. He wiped it against the leg of his jungle fatigues and looked at it again. The whole thing was full of muck. He'd have to clean each round separately.

As he jammed it into the bandolier, there was a noise near him. He glanced up and to the left. A shadow passed him, heading from the direction of the enemy. Sinclair kept his eyes focused on the position of the enemy soldier and slowly drew his combat knife.

The VC moved and Sinclair saw him for the first time. He leaned his rifle against the trunk of the tree and moved forward slowly, quietly, his eyes on the back of the man's head. The man stood once and Sinclair froze. Around him was the sound of the firefight: weapons ripping at each other, bullets snapping through the air to smash into the trees, stripping bark and leaves from them.

As the VC settled back, searching for another target, Sinclair crept closer. Just as the man stood up, Sinclair leaped. He grabbed the man under the chin, lifting his head. As he did, he slashed with his knife, cutting deep. He felt the knife slide through the soft flesh. The enemy grunted in surprise and then sagged. Blood splashed, filling the air with a coppery smell, and then the bowel released, overpowering the copper.

Sinclair rolled the enemy to the right so that he fell

facedown. He grabbed the AK, thinking he would prevent the enemy from recovering it. Then, out of the foliage to the right, another enemy appeared. Sinclair whirled toward him and pulled the trigger of the AK. The muzzle flash, bright in the darkness of the jungle, stabbed out.

The rounds took the soldier in the chest, driving him back. He stumbled and fell, dropping his rifle. Then, before Sinclair could move, a second soldier appeared, firing. Sinclair dived to the right, rolled and fired again, but he missed and the VC vanished. He could hear him, but couldn't see him. Using the sound to aim, Sinclair emptied the magazine.

There was no return fire. Sinclair crawled toward the body of the man he had killed. There was blood on the chest pouch that had turned sticky already. Flies had found the open wound and were buzzing around it.

Keeping his eyes on the section of jungle where the enemy soldier hid, Sinclair tried to pull a magazine free of the blood-soaked pouch. He put his hand in the man's blood, a warm and sticky liquid. He ignored it and got the magazine.

Just as he slammed it home, the VC appeared, standing in a shaft of sunlight that looked like a spotlight. Sinclair pulled the bolt and then fired. He watched the man hit by two, three, four rounds. They ripped into his chest, opening holes. Blood spurted and the man dropped in a loose-boned way that Sinclair had seen before. The VC was dead before he hit the ground.

Then, before he had a chance to move, the firing broke out all around him. No longer was it ten, twelve men shooting at one another. Now there were fifty or sixty of them. He could hear them shouting to each other in Vietnamese. They were crashing through the jungle, pushing toward him.

Sinclair realized that he had run into something more than a simple ambush. Ten, twelve men with a machine gun made up an ambush; this was a platoon that was attacking him. It was too late to get out. The open ground behind him, the rice paddy, would become a killing ground if he tried to escape.

He slipped to the ground and crawled toward a large tree, away from the bodies of the men he had killed. There was a slight depression under the branches and Sinclair crawled into it. He clutched the AK to his chest, almost as if it was an infant that needed protection.

Around him, he could hear the firefight. Weapons on full auto. Grenades, shouts, cries and groans. Men were moving forward, firing single shot or on full auto. The sound rose and fell like the surf hitting a beach.

It was all over, he was sure. He'd led his men into an ambush, surprising the enemy, but then the VC had managed to get more men into the fight, cutting him and his squad off. There was no escape.

Lieutenant Boyson crouched in the filthy water and mud at the side of the rice paddy dike, his eyes almost level with the ground. He had watched the artillery fall into the trees, tearing up the ground and throwing it into the air in great geysers of dirt, smoke and debris. Dust and smoke hung just above the trees. Sinclair and his men swept to the finger of jungle, halted momentarily, and then disappeared.

There was shooting from the trees, first a single burst of a machine gun and then more, as both sides tried to destroy each other. The firing tapered and the lieutenant was about to order the rest of the platoon forward, but then things changed. The firing increased, and the lieutenant realized that most of the shooting was being done by AKs.

The RTO crawled through the water until he was near the lieutenant. He looked up at the officer and asked, "What are you going to do?"

The lieutenant refused to look at the man. He stared at the trees where he could see nothing other than the deep greens of the wall of vegetation. He felt the sweat drip from his face and felt it roll down his sides. He was aware of the small things around him, fighting to break his concentration because he didn't know what he was going to do. With his own men in the trees, he couldn't call in artillery as Sergeant Sinclair had done, and he didn't want to charge the trees because of the open ground in front of him. The truth was that he didn't know what to do and suddenly wished that he'd never seen the ad in the college paper that said he could earn cash in ROTC while attending regular classes.

"Lieutenant," said the RTO, "we've got to do something."

Without thinking about it, the lieutenant leaped to his feet. He waved his arm in the classic motion of the infantry officer and yelled, "Follow me."

He started forward, leaping one rice paddy dike and trying to run to the jungle. Around him, the men got to their feet, obeying the order but not liking it. They began a surging charge across the open ground, shouting like the rebels as they hit the Federal lines at Gettysburg.

And then the jungle erupted, the firing bursting through the vegetation, ripping holes in the curtain of green. Several men stumbled and fell. Others dived for cover, firing their weapons without aiming, burning through their magazines and then lying still, hoping that the enemy wouldn't see them as they hugged the ground.

The lieutenant realized that his assault was drying up and he would be the only one to reach the jungle, if he didn't take a bullet first. He leaped for cover and glanced around as the men fired sporadically. The shooting from the trees tapered until only the RPD was firing and then that stopped too. The lieutenant waited for the assault he was sure that the enemy would mount and wondered what he should do about it. He was aware of his platoon, scattered around him with no semblance of a defensive perimeter. The men were lying where they had taken cover, some of them firing into the jungle, but most of them afraid to shoot because of the squad that was in there.

His nightmare had finally come true. He was pinned down in the open with no idea how he was going to get out. If he looked, he could see the bodies of some of his men, lying facedown near the trees. And all he could do was wait and hope that it would be quick and merciful when it came.

It wasn't much of a plan, but then, it was all that he had.

2

Navy lieutenant Mark Tynan sat in the newly redecorated office of Commander Walker at the Nha Be Navy Base just south of Saigon. Tynan was a fairly tall man, standing over six feet. He had brown hair, cut short now that he was back in South Vietnam, and light blue eyes. The skin of his angular face was tanned a deep brown by the time spent in the tropics —not just South Vietnam, but also in Central America and in Africa. He had been a member of the Navy's elite and secret SEALs almost from the moment he joined the Navy, suffering through all the indignities that the training could offer from Hell Week through the rather subdued, official graduation ceremonies.

Now he sat in the plywood-paneled outer office, watching a clerk pound on an old Underwood typewriter. There was a battleship gray desk, a couple of beat-up couches for visitors to use while they waited, and there were fresh copies of *Stars and Stripes*, *Time*, and *Newsweek*. Hanging on the walls were captured weapons and watercolors painted by local artists. Overhead a fan turned slowly, doing nothing to dispel the heat.

There was a chirping on the clerk's desk and he picked up the field phone sitting there. He said nothing and when he cradled it, he nodded at Tynan. "You may go in."

Tynan entered the inner office and stopped to close the door. The interior was cool because of the air conditioner built into the wall below the window. The blinds were drawn to keep out the sunlight and heat. Like the outer office, the walls were plywood, scorched with a blowtorch to bring out the grain, and then varnished over. Other than a single AK-47 mounted like a trophy fish, the walls were bare.

Walker, a short, rotund man with thick wavy hair sprinkled with gray, sat behind the desk. He had massive eyebrows that looked like furry caterpillars, a round face with a pointed nose, and a thick coarse beard that required him to either shave twice a day or else look as if someone had painted his chin blue-gray.

As Tynan entered, Walker stood up and held out a hand. "Haven't seen you in a long time," he said.

Tynan moved forward, shook Walker's hand, and then waited. When Walker gestured at one of the two chairs sitting in front of his desk, Tynan sank into the closer.

Walker sat down again, shuffled the papers littering his desk, and then stuck them in a drawer so that they were out of sight. He steepled his fingers and touched the underside of his chin. Grinning, he asked, "What do you know about COSVN?"

"Not much," said Tynan. "That's the mythical communist headquarters directing operations of the VC and the NVA in South Vietnam."

"Now why would you call it mythical?"

"Just sounds like the stories of the lost cities of gold or the fountain of youth. Legends that caused men to waste their lives in search of something that doesn't exist. There were rumors, maps, legends, but nothing to prove that any of that ever existed."

"Well," said Walker, smiling, "I think the lost cities of gold did exist. They weren't made of gold, but they did exist."

"Then you're saying that COSVN exists," said Tynan.

Walker rubbed a hand over his chin and then stared up at the slowly revolving fan. "I think that intelligence estimates we're getting from the Parrot's Beak region around Tay Ninh suggest that it does. Now, the problem has been that we've assumed that it's on the South Vietnamese side of the border. The location has been pegged as close to Cu Chi or Dau Tieng or in the Hobo Woods. Now it seems that it's just on the other side of the border, in Cambodia."

Tynan nodded and asked, "Just what in the hell does this have to do with me?"

Walker waved a hand and said, "Bear with me for a moment and we'll get to that." He stood up and moved to the window but didn't open the blind. He stared at it, his hands clasped behind his back. Finally he turned.

"The Navy's role in this war hasn't been as great as we'd like it to be. We participate in the air war over North Vietnam, when we're allowed to. We patrol the coasts looking for infiltrations of weapons and men, but that is a policeman's task, not the role for the most powerful navy on the face of the Earth. We have some patrol boats operating on the various waterways, but the real war is being fought on the land by the Army and the Marines."

Tynan listened to the lecture with a growing sense of apprehension. He knew what was coming and tried to think of a way to dodge it but nothing came to mind.

"Now, the Army had a platoon run into some trouble near Parrot's Beak a couple of days ago. Walked into what seemed to be a normal ambush and then found themselves facing a much larger force."

"Just like the Army to walk into an ambush," said Tynan.

"No, this really wasn't typical. From what I've learned, they handled themselves professionally. The VC had a full company, outnumbering our guys three, four to one."

"Interesting," said Tynan, "but what does it have to do with anything?"

Walker returned to his chair and said, "I have been all around the subject, haven't I? Well, it's all connected when I get to the point."

He opened the middle drawer of his desk and pulled out a map. He pointed to it and waited until Tynan stood up and moved to the desk where he could see.

"Latest intelligence reports have put the COSVN in the Parrot's Beak region. This ambush, by more men than we suspected to be in the vicinity, has convinced us that the VC have something important in that area."

Tynan shook his head. "That's a little thin."

"No one said it was going to be easy," snapped Walker. "I'm giving you everything we have. Something is building up there. Couple that with the intelligence reports and it gives us the COSVN."

"Just what's the nature of these reports?"

Walker leaned back and steepled his fingers again. "Some of it comes from our agents—Vietnamese working for us. Some of it comes from ELINT, meaning people sniffers and a monitoring of radio signals in the area. And some of it comes from the Army's ground forces and helicopter pilots. Things they've seen and reported through channels. Added together, it becomes a fairly weighty package."

"Okay, what does that have to do with me?"

Walker waved at the chair, indicating that Tynan was to sit down again. "I want you to take a team up there and pinpoint the COSVN. Once we've accomplished that, we turn the data over to the Army and let them beat the hell out of the enemy." Walker grinned again and added, "I know what you're thinking, but it really would be a Navy victory. We hand them everything on a silver platter."

"And if the COSVN is not there?"

"Don't worry about that, it is. We know it. It's just a question of locating it precisely."

Tynan knew that there was no way to refuse the mission without looking like a coward. Staring at the map that was sitting on the desk, he could see that there was jungle and open ground. Swamp and rice fields. Just about every kind of terrain except mountains. Places to hide and places that were as open as a parade ground. Places that divisions could elude detection and places where a single man could be seen for miles. But then, it was an interesting question. Could the enemy hide a major—*the* major—headquarters in the vicinity and escape detection by everything and everyone that the Americans could bring into the search? Could he locate it when no one else had been able to do the job?

"How many men do I get for the job?"

"How many men would you want?"

"No more than six. Radio operator, a medic, and a weapons expert."

"What about a guide?"

"No," said Tynan, shaking his head. "No."

"Not Vietnamese. This would be an American who has been in the area."

"No," said Tynan again. "If he's so good, why didn't he find the headquarters in the first place?"

"Part of the reason that we're convinced the COSVN is in that area is the report he made."

"What's his training?"

"Regular Army. . ."

"Christ, that's no training at all. They teach them which end of the barrel the bullet comes out, tell them to take salt tablets and not drink all their water at once, and think they've got a jungle fighter."

"Well," said Walker, "you've got him and you're going to have to take care of him."

For a moment Tynan was silent. Then he nodded once, realizing that orders were orders and although Walker might envision this as some kind of coup for the Navy, the Army would say that it led the SEALs in and then had to support them with more men once contact had been made. It was not the best way to operate.

"Any other bits of information you'd care to share with me?"

"No," said Walker, "that'll about do it. Oh, except that you'll be leaving here inside of two days. The brass in Saigon would like to eliminate this nuisance as quickly as possible."

"Terrific," said Tynan as he stood to leave.

Sinclair had lain quietly as the Vietcong and the North Vietnamese set about catching and killing all the Americans who had entered the jungle with him. There were periodic shots and shouts. Commands in Vietnamese and curses in English. He heard an M16 on full auto rip through a magazine. AKs opened up all around him. A single explosion from a hand grenade punctuated the brief, fierce firefight.

From the growing number of AKs firing and from the shouting in Vietnamese, Sinclair knew that they had walked into it. The enemy had been waiting, driven to ground by the artillery that hadn't been adequate to eliminate them. That was the problem with the war: too many times the enemy had fooled everyone by being where he wasn't supposed to be.

Now all Sinclair could do was hug the ground and not move, praying that the enemy wouldn't make a thorough search. When night fell, if the enemy was spread thin enough, he might be able to slip away. He'd move deeper into the jungle, using the vegetation to hide him from the enemy.

The number of M16s firing tapered. Then there were only occasional shots from the M16 as the survivors tried to get out before they were killed. Sinclair wrapped himself around the spiny trunk of the bush and tried to see what was going on. He could smell the dank staleness of the jungle floor and the rotting vegetation. Sweat dampened him, trickling down his back to send chills up his spine. He imagined scorpions and spiders crawling on his bare skin but ignored the sensations. To give in would be to give himself away.

In the distance he heard one of his men surrender, throwing away his weapon and shouting, "Don't shoot. Don't shoot."

There was more shouting in Vietnamese and then a single scream. A moment later the voice said, "Please. I surrender."

Sinclair strained to see what was going on but didn't want to give himself away. As the last of the shooting stopped, he knew that each of his men was dead, had surrendered, or were in hiding like he was. There was nothing he could do for anyone now. The intelligent thing was to lie still and wait for nightfall.

The voice, which he couldn't recognize, pleaded: "Don't shoot me. I surrender."

That brought laughter from the Vietnamese. A single shot sounded and Sinclair thought that the enemy had killed their prisoner. But then the voice came again: "Don't shoot me. I know things to help you."

For an instant, Sinclair was sickened, but then realized that in a similar situation he'd tell the enemy anything to keep them from shooting him. He'd lie about what he might know, hoping that they would take him to a camp to be interrogated. Once there, he'd have a better chance of surviving. So far the captured soldier hadn't told them anything.

There was a sudden crashing to his left, and he slowly turned his head. A single sandal-clad foot appeared near his face, inches from his nose. The man squatted down to examine the ground. He picked up an expanded round and put it into his pocket. Sinclair could smell the man. He could see the sweat stains under his arms but couldn't see his head or face. Finally the enemy stood and moved away. Had Sinclair wanted to, he could have tripped him.

He listened to the Vietcong torment the man they had captured. They slapped him around, laughing about it. There were single shots and each time that happened, Sinclair was sure the man had been killed. But each time, the voice came again, asking not to be killed.

As he lay there, hidden from the enemy who didn't seem to be searching for anyone, he wondered what the lieutenant was doing. When the firing stopped, he should have known that his own men were either dead or captured, and called in the artillery again. If his own men had survived, they would have appeared at the edge of the jungle to let him know. The poor, green bastard was afraid to do anything.

The enemy swept by, toward the edge of the jungle, moving cautiously to the curtain of vegetation so that they could look out on the Americans crouched in the rice paddies. Firing began again. AKs on full auto, an RPD, and then M16s answering. Sinclair heard some of the bullets snap through the air over his head.

As quickly as it started, it ended. The VC who had been firing at the Americans withdrew from the edge of the jungle and began to take ambush positions. Obviously, they hoped that a retreat would draw the Americans into the jungle where they could be cut to ribbons and killed quickly.

Sinclair didn't move. He hugged the ground and the trunk of the tree, waiting for the dark and praying that the lieutenant wouldn't get the rest of the platoon killed in some stupid, grandstand move.

* * *

Tynan entered the club. It wasn't much of a club. A wooden building with two huge floor fans roaring, trying to cool the interior. It was dark inside. There were a few tables and some chairs. A bar made of wood salvaged from ammo crates and shipping packages stood along one wall. A mirror, cracked on one side and with a bullet hole in the middle, was fastened to the wall behind the bar. A single Vietnamese woman worked the bar, ignoring most of the sailors in the club.

Tynan spotted his men sitting at a table close to the fan. One of them, Thomas Jones, had been with Tynan in Vietnam before. He was a young man with blond hair, blue eyes and a fondness for Hershey's chocolate. Jones was a wizard with the radio, able to repair in seconds what would take most men a day to do. He hadn't liked Navy life, figuring it was too easy for an armed force, and then had fallen in love with the SEALs. It was exactly the tough fighting force that Jones had wanted.

Next to him was a man Tynan had met earlier in the day. Jonathan Wentworth was thin and short, with black hair cut close. He had sharp features, a big nose, and small, brown eyes. He didn't look like he could hold his own, yet had graduated from the school at Coronado, California, and that meant that he was a man who could do his job.

Sitting on the other side of the table was Bruce Cummings, a small man with light hair and light eyes. He had a face that could get lost in the crowd. There was nothing outstanding about him except that he had a mustache. Most SEALs didn't have any facial hair because of the SCUBA gear they were required to use. The mustache didn't look very old.

Tynan pulled out a wicker chair and dropped into it, leaning forward so that he could talk to the men. Each of them had a beer, and there was an empty glass waiting for Tynan. Jones filled it and then waited.

Tynan took a drink and then said, "We're going out in the next day or so."

"Good," said Jones. "I was getting tired of hanging around here anyway."

Tynan glanced over his shoulder, saw that the bar girl had taken no notice of him. There was no one close to them. He lowered his voice and then said, "Looks like we're going to Cambodia."

"Good," repeated Jones. "I haven't been there yet. One more country to add to the list of places I've visited."

Tynan shook his head and said, "I wish that I could share your enthusiasm for international travel."

"What's the deal, Skipper?" asked Cummings.

"We'll have a full-blown briefing later, but for now I think we'd better start thinking in terms of hitting the field." He glanced at the pitcher of beer sitting in the middle of the table.

"You're not going to tell us that we can't drink this, are you?" asked Wentworth.

"No. But I am going to tell you that we don't want to drink much more of it. We haven't been officially alerted, but I think we'll get that in the next couple of hours." He took a drink and asked, "Where're Jacobs and Hernandez?"

"Went in search of women," said Jones. "Said that they would be around here if we needed them in short order."

"They give any indication of where they were

going to find these women?" asked Tynan.

"No sir. Just indicated that they probably wouldn't be round-eyes because there are no round-eyes handy. Lots of Vietnamese though, some of whom are not adverse to picking up a little spare change in the act of love," said Jones.

Tynan drained his beer and then wiped the foam from his lip with his hand. He sat back in his chair, ignored the heat and humidity of the stagnant air in the club. "That's about the quickest way to catch something that we don't need to take with us into the jungle."

Now Jones said, "That's why I spend my money on chocolate. Doesn't give you diseases."

"No," said Wentworth, "but it's not nearly as much fun."

"If you men are through with your discussion of the relative merits of various vices, I might have some instructions for each of you."

"Sorry, Skipper," said Jones.

"Walker didn't give me a real-time frame, but we can figure on leaving here inside of forty-eight hours. He's hot to get this thing on the road and will push to see that it gets moving. I would suggest that we take maybe an hour to relax now, and then get at it. Wentworth, I want you to find Jacobs and Hernandez and get them back for a briefing at, say, nineteen hundred. Jones, you find us some commo equipment. Cummings, you check into the medical supplies and see if there's anything we'll need. Questions?"

"Yeah, Skipper," said Wentworth. "Why do I have to go find Jacobs and Hernandez?"

"Because," said Tynan, laughing, "I figure you'll

have the best chance of locating them because of your familiarity with the locals."

"I don't know if that is a compliment or not," said Wentworth.

"Neither do I," agreed Tynan. He hesitated and then said, "Let's get at it."

3

The lieutenant, his uniform soaked, knelt in the corner of the rice paddy and studied the tree line. The firing that had poured from it slowed and stopped. His men, who had returned the fire, quit shooting.

The lieutenant reached up and wiped the sweat from his face. He pulled his steel pot lower, as if to protect his eyebrows, and tried to see the enemy soldiers. There were shadowy movements behind the thick branches of the bushes and the lacy leaves of the ferns, but the lieutenant wouldn't allow his platoon to fire. He was afraid he might kill some of his own men.

Finally, unable to decide what to do, he crawled to the RTO and took the handset. He rolled to his back, his head below the level of the rice paddy dike. For a moment he stayed there, staring up into the cloudless sky, just as he had seen Sinclair doing. The plan hit him at once and he cursed himself for not thinking about it earlier.

He keyed the mike and said, "Any Army Aviation unit, this is Red Rider one six."

"Red Rider one six, this is Blackhawk one two."

"Roger, one two, we are in contact and need an aviation assist."

"Say nature of assist."

"Roger. We have men pinned down in a tree line and need assistance to free them and to spot the enemy."

"Roger, one six. Wait one."

The lieutenant wiped his face on the back of his hand and took a deep breath. It was so simple. Get some helicopters and get the men out of the trees. At the very least, provide them with some cover.

"One six, this is Blackhawk one two. Be advised that you are to contact Talon three three on forty-two decimal five. They will lend gun support. Do you require medivac assistance?"

The lieutenant had seen two men fall into the rice paddy water near the tree line but neither of them had moved since they were hit. He was convinced they were dead. But there was a possibility that there were wounded in the trees.

"Roger."

"Say coordinates."

The lieutenant could have kicked himself. He should have thought of that himself. They couldn't find him if he didn't provide the coordinates. He gave them and then was told to contact the guns.

Before the RTO could change frequencies, he heard the distant pop of rotor blades. He sat up enough to search the sky to the south and saw a speck that might be the first of the helicopters.

When the tuning squeal died, he said, "Talon three three, this is Red Rider one six."

"Go."

"Have you spotted south of our location."

"Roger. Can you throw smoke?"

The lieutenant glanced at the RTO, who was already pulling a smoke grenade from his harness. He jerked the pin free and then threw the grenade toward the tree line.

"We are south of the smoke," said the lieutenant.

"Roger. ID yellow smoke."

"Roger yellow smoke."

"Are there friendlies in the trees?"

The lieutenant again looked at the RTO and wondered what he should say. There were friendlies in the tree lines but he didn't know if they were alive or not.

"Negative friendlies," he said. When the RTO started to protest, he held up a hand and shook his head.

"Roger," said the gunship pilot. "Rolling in."

The noise from the helicopters changed then, the engine roaring and the blades popping with the stresses of the gun run. From the rear of the rocket pods came the sporadic puffs of smoke as the rocket engines ignited. The rockets leaped from the helicopter and then dropped, slamming into the trees. As the lead ship broke, the door gunners opened fire with their M60s, raking the trees with a devastating fire. At the same moment, the second aircraft opened fire, protecting the first.

"Yeah!" yelled the lieutenant. "Yeah."

As the gunships began working the finger of jungle, four men leaped up and tried to sprint across the rice paddies. They dodged right and left, leaping and jogging, trying to evade enemy fire as they raced to the men who were sprawled short of the trees. Over them the gunships kept up the pressure.

Two of them reached one of the downed men, each grabbing an arm. Together they lifted, pulling him to the rear as fast as they could move. His head was down, his helmet forgotten as they dragged him from the water. No one bothered to search for his weapon, lost in the rice paddy.

As soon as they got to the rice paddy dike, they rolled him over it and then dived over with him. One of them shoved a hand inside the wounded man's jungle fatigue jacket and then shook his head. The man was dead before they could get to him.

The second pair reached the second fallen soldier as firing broke out from the jungle. They both dropped into the water, taking the little cover they could find. As that happened, the gunships rolled in again, the mini-guns on the lead ship firing in short bursts that sounded like a buzz saw and cut through the jungle with the same deadly speed.

The firing fell off then and the two men dragged the wounded soldier to the rear. Neither of them worried about hurting the man. They could tell from the wound in the throat and the waxy look of the skin that the man was dead.

As the second two men got back to their lines, the lieutenant was on the radio again. "Medivac, medivac, this is Red Rider one six."

"One six, this is Blackhawk one two. Go."

"Roger. Need medivac for two. And then we'll need slicks for extraction."

"Roger. Extraction."

* * *

It was almost dusk when Tynan made it to the briefing room being used for the mission. A small room with air-conditioning, a table in the center of it, and nothing on the walls other than a single map of the Parrot's Beak region of South Vietnam. Walker stood near the map, his hands behind his back, and stared at the men seated in the chairs surrounding the table.

Wentworth had been successful in finding both Jacobs and Hernandez: they were sitting on the same side of the table with him. Tynan sat down opposite them and waited for Walker to start.

"Gentlemen," he said, "here's the deal. A covert mission into Cambodia, here, near Parrot's Beak. A simple sneak-and-peek job to locate an enemy head-quarters so that the Army can eliminate it."

He glanced at Tynan and said, "Oh, you'll be glad to know that your Army guide has opted out. Brass decided that there was no need for him."

"Good," said Tynan. "They were right about not needing him, not to mention that he'd probably get in the way."

Walker nodded and then looked at the faces of each of the men around the table. Satisfied that he had their attention, he began again, talking about the need for this mission and the coup it would represent. The elimination of the COSVN would be a feather in the caps of all who participated in the destruction, and it could mean medals and promotions for all of them. More important, it would be a demoralizing event for the Vietcong and the North Vietnamese. It would mean that nothing was invulnerable, if the Americans decided to attack it. The mission could shorten the war and there wasn't a

man in the room who didn't want the war short-
ened.

When he had finished with his pep talk, he looked
at Tynan and said, "Lieutenant, is there anything that
you wanted to address here?"

Tynan got to his feet and looked at the men he had
assembled. It was a well-balanced team with men
who were specialists in different areas. Weapons,
demolitions, radio, and medicine. There wasn't much
that he could have done to improve the team with the
exception of adding an intell specialist, but there
wasn't a real need for that.

Tynan started by saying, "You each know what
has to be done, what equipment we'll need. I don't
have to go over that, and don't want to, unless
there is something special that one of you would
like to discuss."

Slowly, he looked into the faces of the men, but
none of them seemed to have any ideas. "All right,
we talked about assignments this afternoon. We know
where we're going, so we can plan accordingly."

"Skipper," said Jacobs. "How long we going to be
in the field?"

"No more than one week. We locate the COSVN
faster than that, we can get out."

"Walking or riding?" asked Jones.

Tynan looked at the map. "Army aviation has
assets at Tay Ninh, Dau Tieng, Cu Chi, and Muc
Hoa, all of which could have helos in to us within an
hour of the call."

Walker interrupted here. "The Army will not cross
the Cambodian border. You'll have to be on this side
of it to get them in there."

"So we walk and then we ride," said Tynan.

"Which leads to my second question," said Jones.

"What if we step into the shit on the other side of the border?"

Tynan looked at Walker, who shrugged and said, "I would think that if you were in deep shit, there'd be someone to cross over to help you out."

"The solution," said Tynan, "is to keep the enemy from seeing us."

The conversation settled down then. Each of the men had been prepared to head into the field on an hour's notice. If there was something unusual about the mission, they would have had to adjust to that, but this one didn't have any special features. A quiet search of a specific area and then a silent retreat with the information in hand.

Walker took over then, telling them that Army Aviation would be available to put them into the LZ in the morning. That would give them the day to get out and under cover so that the enemy might not know that they were around.

"Seems to me," said Jacobs, "that if we can get someone to make a phantom pickup late in the day, we have an even better chance of being undetected. Makes Charlie think that we left. Go in at dawn, out at dusk."

"Good point," said Walker. "I'll see what I can arrange on that."

Tynan looked at the men and asked, "Anything else that any of you want to ask?"

One by one, the men shook their heads. Finally Jacobs asked, "What time we take off tomorrow?"

Tynan looked at Walker, who shrugged and asked, "What time would you like to go in?"

Tynan rubbed his chin. The last thing he wanted was to call attention to himself and his men. "What time do the sweep-and-destroy missions deploy?"

"Unless there's something unusual going on, I'd say first lifts in about zero eight hundred and then follow-ons as fast as the helos can move the men around throughout the day."

"Flight from here to Tay Ninh takes what? An hour or so? Pickup on the pier at zero seven three zero. That'll give us a good night's sleep before we hit the field."

"Helos will be waiting. Anything else?"

When no one spoke, Tynan said, "Then I'll see you tomorrow morning."

It was also at dusk that the flight of helicopters was orbiting just south of the finger of jungle where the firefight had taken place. The dead and wounded had been evacked and although there had been no return fire from the jungle for over thirty minutes, no one was making any plans to enter it. That would have to be accomplished in the morning, when they would have the whole day to learn the fate of the squad that had attacked into it earlier.

The gunships circled over the top of them like vultures waiting for something to die. Periodically, one of the door gunners fired into the darkened jungle, trying to entice the enemy to return fire, but if Charlie was still there, he wasn't shooting.

As the last of the sun disappeared, the slicks came in from the west, shooting an approach so that the lead helo dropped his skids into the rice paddy water no more than ten feet from the first group of men. With the rotor wash pushing the water toward the rice paddy dikes in small waves, the lieutenant led his men to the rear of the helos. They leaped up and in, smearing the clean deck with the mud and slime from their boots and their uniforms.

When the trail aircraft was loaded, the flight lifted off, the door gunners firing into the trees. The muzzle flashes reached out, stabbing into the onrushing night. Ruby-colored tracers flashed, lacing out and then tumbling into the sky. There was no indication that the enemy was still in the jungle or that Sinclair and his men had survived the afternoon.

The lieutenant, sitting on the floor, his mud-caked M16 held in his left hand, leaned out, looking to the rear. He could see little other than the charcoal of the jungle and the gray of the rice paddies to the south. Nine men were lost in there and he had done nothing to help them.

He turned and looked at the men in the helicopter with him. They were all staring at him and he could see the hate in their eyes. They all knew that any one of them could have been one of the men left behind. Each of them knew that the lieutenant was incompetent. Couldn't figure out how to get to the jungle to help the men there. And if he couldn't do that, then there were probably a lot of other things that he couldn't do. They were all probably wondering when his incompetence would kill the rest of them.

He wanted to say he was sorry. He'd learned a great deal while crouched in that rice paddy, but the men wouldn't want to hear that. ROTC and the Army's basic school for infantry officers hadn't taught him how to survive in the jungle with bullets flying around. He was just beginning to understand that. Just beginning to learn that.

Now the task would be impossible because his men wouldn't trust him. They would know that he left nine men in the jungle. He didn't run out and leave them. He didn't panic and make stupid mistakes. He had just stayed where he was, muddy water staining his uniform, and done nothing.

Over the roar of the wind and the pop of the rotors, he shouted, "Tomorrow we'll go back."

But he knew that it was too little too late. He should have done something when the firing had broken out all around them that afternoon.

As he had hidden in the bushes, he had been sure that the rockets and then the machine-gun fire from the helicopter gunships was going to kill him before the enemy could find him. But somehow he had survived that. The rockets hadn't come close and when the mini-guns had begun to rain down, the bullets had been aimed deeper into the jungle. He had lucked out all the way around.

Now it was dark. The last of the helicopters had gone thirty minutes, an hour ago. He hadn't heard a Vietnamese voice for two hours. There was almost no sound in the jungle. It was as if the Americans had killed every living thing around him. Even the insects were gone.

Slowly he crawled from under the bush. His muscles were stiff from the hours of enforced inactivity. His bladder hurt him but he hadn't wanted to take a chance of losing his life because he couldn't hold it for a while. Now, with the jungle around him empty, he could relieve himself.

He stood up and stepped to a huge teak tree that had taken a machine-gun burst about head high. The ripped bark was evident even in the dark.

He stood there for a moment, then opened his fly. As he relieved himself, he leaned forward, his head against his forearm. He tried to make no noise and he

tried not to sigh. In the jungle even the smallest of
pleasures was important.

Finished, he had no idea of his next move. He'd
lost his M16 in the firefight, but still had the AK he'd
taken from the body of an enemy soldier. By now, he
was sure that the enemy would have carried off their
dead so that he'd have no luck finding more ammo.
The enemy was very good at leaving nothing for the
Americans to exploit.

For a moment he crouched there, listening to the
jungle. There was a musty odor from the pool he had
created. There was a stench from rotting vegetation.
And there was a wetness, from the humidity. And no
relief from the heat. Even with the sun gone, it was
hot and miserable in the jungle.

"Okay," said Sinclair out loud. He shut up, startled
by the sound of his own voice. Jungle survival required that he be as quiet as possible. Sounds carried
well in the jungle. People thought that the vegetation
would deaden the sound, but it wasn't quite true.
Sometimes sounds carried a long way.

The nighttime jungle offered him some protection.
Only a little light from the stars and the moon could
filter through the dense vegetation. He could move a
long way without seeing or hearing anyone else. He
could find himself four, five, six clicks away at
dawn. Then he could move out into the open and wait
for an Army helicopter crew to spot him.

He began to move then, slowly, carefully, feeling
the ground in front of him with his toe and then setting his foot down easily, careful not to snap any
twigs or kick any trip wires. It was a hard way to
walk. His senses were strained as he listened to
everything around him. He sniffed the air, searching
for the smoke of a cigarette or the odor of a human

body that would tell him that there was another human somewhere close.

For thirty minutes he worked his way through the jungle, making no sound. He felt guilty about leaving the scene of the firefight without checking to see if the others were dead, but there was nothing he could do for them. The squad had been scattered too wide for him to be able to help any of his friends. The lieutenant should have taken care of that, but the kid didn't know what he was doing. It would take another month before he would understand the finer points of the Vietnam War.

Sinclair shook himself. He couldn't let his mind wander. He had to concentrate on what he was doing. He had to keep his mind focused on moving through the jungle because he couldn't afford another mistake. He'd made his quota already.

Finally he stopped and crouched at the base of a giant teak tree, its roots sticking up through the jungle floor like the gnarled fingers of an arthritic hand. He closed his eyes and felt the sweat bead and drip down his face. He needed a drink but there wasn't much water left in his canteen and he wanted to save it for later when he'd need it more.

As he stood up to begin again, he heard a bolt slide forward to his left. He turned to face that direction slowly but saw nothing there. As he stared into the dark, he felt the warm metal of a rifle barrel pressed against the side of his neck. He took a deep breath, exhaled, and then quietly said, "I hope you're an American."

The answer he got was in Vietnamese and he knew that he was screwed.

4

Tynan was standing at the edge of the pier that stretched out into the Saigon River on the south side of Nha Be. It was a wide, muddy river and on the opposite bank were the beginnings of a swamp that stretched southwest for miles. Bunches of trees punctuated the skyline. To the west were dark clouds that suggested rain later in the day.

"Equipment is all on hand, Skipper," said Jacobs.

Tynan turned and looked back to where the rest of the team stood waiting. There wasn't much in the way of equipment. Weapons and rucksacks, radios and battery packs and little more. Sneak-and-peek operations didn't demand much.

Beyond the edge of the pier, made of thick wooden planks that oozed sap and were stained with tar, there were short, corrugated tin buildings to one side and a tree line along the bank on the other. On the road that led to the pier, there was a jeep coming at them raising a cloud of red dust, and Tynan recognized Walker as the driver.

"Well, shit," said Tynan to no one in particular. "I wonder what's happened now?"

Jacobs turned and saw Walker as he stopped the jeep and climbed out. "Maybe the mission has been scrubbed."

"I wouldn't bet the family farm on it." Tynan walked across the pier to the jeep. "Morning, Commander."

"Good morning. You all set?"

"Just waiting on the helos. Once they arrive we'll toss our gear into the rear and we'll be off."

"Good. Good." Walker looked down, as if he'd found something fascinating on the pier. "Got one other problem."

"Yes sir," said Tynan. "I suspected things were going too easily."

"You'll make a stop at Tay Ninh and pick up an Army lieutenant named Boyson. Yesterday, he was out in the area you'll be going into and might provide some help, having had that fresh a look around there."

"I thought we'd decided that any such assistance would be of very little use to us and might compromise the whole mission."

Walker stared into Tynan's eyes. "The point is not open to debate. You'll take the lieutenant with you."

Tynan took a deep breath and asked, "Why is it that the Navy goes to all the trouble to train highly skilled special forces personnel and then destroys their capability by saddling them with people who have neither the training nor the stamina to stay with us?"

"The decision was not made by the Navy," said Walker.

Tynan understood then. Command decisions made at MACV weren't open to question. Soldiers, sailors, and marines were moved at the whim of generals who didn't understand the nature of the Vietnam War or the tactics of guerrilla operations.

"Yes sir. Lieutenant Boyson at Tay Ninh."

"You'll have to refuel there anyway. He'll be standing by at the POL when you arrive."

Before Tynan could react, there was the beat of helicopter rotors in the distance. Tynan put a hand to his eyes to shade them and saw the flight of two helos coming at him from the east. They were a hundred, two hundred feet over the surface of the water, aimed at the pier.

Walker held out a hand. "Good luck, Lieutenant. See you in about a week or so."

"Thank you, sir." Tynan turned and shouted, "Let's get ready."

The men moved to the equipment, picking it up. They struggled into the rucksacks and then moved off to the dirt near the edge of the pier to give the helos the room to land. As the lead aircraft approached, the nose coming up and the rotor wash blowing forward to hit them like the first gusts of a hurricane, Tynan turned his back. He felt the dust and dirt picked up by the rotor wash strike his spine and shoulders. He closed his eyes and waited.

When both helicopters had landed and the noise from the engines had died, he turned. Without a word from him, the men began moving forward, heads bowed as if afraid the rotors would flex down to kill them. They jogged out onto the pier, tossed their gear into the cargo compartments and then climbed up inside.

Tynan was the last to board. He leaned out, looked at the trail helo, and then turned. He touched the pilot on the shoulder and held up a thumb, signaling the man they were ready to take off.

The aircraft lifted to three feet and hovered there, rocking gently. The rotor wash created a minor dust storm and Tynan lost sight of Walker, his jeep, and the remainder of Nha Be. A moment later, the helo turned and the nose dropped as they charged off the side of the pier. They lost a little altitude, dropping dangerously close to the surface of the river, but then began a rapid climb out. Tynan heard one of his men whoop like he was a cowboy on the back of a bronco.

They continued the climb up to fifteen hundred feet and leveled off. To the right, north, out the cargo compartment door, was the sprawl of Saigon. No tall buildings, but a spread of a city with a few wide boulevards through the center and many narrower streets crisscrossing it. There was a haze over the city, like the smog that would hide Los Angeles, but created by the tropical sun and the high humidity.

To the south was nothing but a huge swamp of grasses barely taller than the surface of the water. Sunlight reflected from it, flashing brightly. A group of huge swamp birds took off, flapping giant wings as they raced along only a few feet above the grass.

They turned then so that Tynan lost sight of the swamp. Now there was solid ground under them along with Highway One. Trucks, jeeps, and oxcarts choked the two-lane blacktop. Now there were coconut, palm, and date trees along the road. Small villages were scattered along it and suddenly off to the right was the huge American base at Cu Chi. It dwarfed the Vietnamese hamlet it was named for.

They continued along the highway and then broke farther to the north. Tynan saw the remains of the bridge at Go Dau Ha lying in the river. There was a road that led down to the bank and it seemed that the Americans had built a ford rather than try to repair the bridge again.

Finally, he saw Nui Ba Den, the huge mountain that stuck up into the air like a single pimple on an otherwise clear face. On the top was an American camp, nearly as large as the complex at Cu Chi. To the southwest of it was the city of Tay Ninh that had nearly a million residents.

"Getting close, Skipper," yelled Jones.

"Yeah, real close," agreed Tynan.

They entered the traffic pattern, landing by hovering down the runway, and then broke to the right so that they could enter the POL. As the aircraft touched down, a single man carrying an M16 and wearing a rucksack broke toward them. He glanced into the rear of the trailing ship and then leaped up into the cargo compartment of the lead craft.

"Where's Tynan?" he asked, shouting over the sound of the engine.

"I'm Tynan. You Boyson?"

"Yeah."

The crew chief had abandoned his position, moved to the other side of the helo, and partially closed the cargo compartment door so that he could get at the fuel tanks.

As that happened, Tynan pulled Boyson to the side and said, "I think the thing for you to do is forget this whole nonsense of going with us."

"What's that mean?"

"We're going to be traveling fast and we're going to be traveling quiet."

"I can handle it."

Tynan shook his head. "You don't understand. This isn't like your normal mission. It's not like the search-and-destroy missions you're used to. We have to move quietly and quickly."

"I can handle it."

"Why don't you do us all a favor and forget about it," shouted Jacobs, interrupting the two officers.

"I don't need some enlisted puke telling me what to do, or not to do," said Boyson, looking first at Jacobs and then back to Tynan.

Tynan just shrugged and turned his attention back to the instrument panel and what he could see through the windshield. It wasn't much: other aircraft at their refueling points, a pilot standing at the rear of a cargo compartment pissing onto the skid, and a huge black fuel blatter that looked as if it would be the perfect target for the VC mortar crews.

The crew chief finished the refueling and pushed the door back into place, locking it there with a cotter pin that would keep it from vibrating forward. Once he climbed into his well behind the M60 machine gun, the sound from the engine increased as the pilot rolled on the throttle. A moment later they were hovering between the refueling points, gathering speed for a takeoff to the south.

As they broke over the perimeter, a line of dark green rubberized sandbags and six strands of coiled concertina, Tynan shouted, "Check your gear and your weapons."

He pulled back the bolt on his CAR-15, making sure he had a round chambered. He flicked on the safety and set the weapon on the deck beside him. He took out his pistol, a Browning M35 that held thirteen rounds in the staggered box magazine and a fourteenth in the chamber. Satisfied that he was ready, he touched the top of the three canteens he wore, making sure that the caps were secure. Water was a resource almost as critical as ammunition in the jungles of Vietnam. A short supply of either could mean a quick and untimely death for the soldier.

The copilot turned, lifted the boom mike of his helmet out of the way, and shouted, "You got an LZ that you want to hit picked out?"

Tynan pulled his map from his jungle fatigue pocket and crouched at the foot of the radio console between the two seats. He showed it to the pilot and yelled, "I'd like to hit this one here."

"No," shouted the pilot, waving both hands almost like an umpire calling the runner safe. "Not good. Charlie has bunkers ringing that place. Not in them much, but we could get shot to hell before we could set down."

That surprised Tynan. He'd thought that the pilots would agree to anything that he came up with. He opened the map up so that it was spread out. "Where'd you recommend?"

The pilot grinned. "Saigon. Failing that"—he pointed to three LZs—"any one of those. Good cover for you on the ground and no evidence of bunkers for the enemy."

Tynan wiped his face and stared at the map. None of the three were very close to where he wanted to be. It would mean a march of six or seven clicks just to get to his starting point. Two, three hours, before he was in an area where he could begin the mission.

He found an open area full of rice paddies, swamp, and fingers of jungle reaching over the border like the hand of a giant trying to drag South Vietnam into Cambodia.

"How about here?" he asked.

"You got a couple of hamlets here and here. The inhabitants have died, but that doesn't mean Charlie hasn't got someone sitting around waiting to report our landing."

"Okay," shouted Tynan, holding down the map so that the wind through the open cargo compartment doors wouldn't yank it away and blow it to the ground. "Can you put us down there, close to the trees?"

"If that's what you want."

Tynan pulled at his bottom lip and then pointed to a small clearing two or three clicks from the LZ. "Could you land here about an hour later?"

The pilot shook his head but didn't refuse. Instead he asked, "Why?"

"If Charlie sees us land here and then an hour later sees the helos come back, he might think that we've been picked up. He'll think we're gone."

"I'm not sure that we'll fool anyone. Charlie'll be able to see that there's no one in the cargo compartment if he's close enough to see us land."

"Then close the doors."

"Then we might as well hang out a sign that says we're trying to be sneaky. We don't normally fly with the doors closed," said the pilot.

"Can you do it?" asked Tynan, exasperated.

"Sure we can do it."

"I'd appreciate it."

"Okay." The pilot took one last look at Tynan's map and then got out his own. He made a couple of marks on the acetate overlay and then pulled the boom mike down. Tynan saw his lips moving as he pointed off to the west. The other pilot nodded and they began a slow bank in that direction.

Tynan turned and looked at his men. Two were sitting on the red troop seat against the transmission wall of the Huey. Another sat on the deck, his feet dangling out the door. The Army lieutenant sat with his M16 across his lap, leaning against the fuselage behind the pilot's seat. He was studying his boots.

"Okay," yelled Tynan. When the men looked at him and leaned closer, he added quickly, "We're about to go in. Let's get ready."

"What's the drill, Skipper?" asked Jacobs.

"Into the trees as fast as we can move and then hold up to get oriented."

"Want me on point?" asked Jacobs.

"If you want to take it, but as I say, just into the trees and then we'll survey the situation before moving too far afield."

"Aye aye, sir."

The crew chief leaned around the corner and shouted, "We're about two out."

Tynan glanced at his men and asked, "Anyone have a last-minute question?" He didn't expect one but felt he had to ask.

No one said a word. Jacobs worked the bolt of his weapon, chambering a round, and then looked out the cargo compartment door.

Tynan shifted so that he could leap out the instant the skids touched the ground. He reached out and grabbed the post behind the pilot's seat. He glanced to the front, through the windshield. There wasn't much to see: jungle and rice paddies and a network of dikes; far off to one side was a single farmer's hootch that had a caved-in roof.

As the helo flared, Tynan called out, "Get ready."

Then, suddenly, they were on the ground. As the skids touched, Tynan leaped out, sinking into the muck. He struggled forward, reaching one of the dikes. He dropped onto the side of it and glanced over his shoulder. Both helos were down and the men were out, moving through the water. As they tried to get to the jungle, both helos lifted. They charged across the ground, and then suddenly the noses came up and both helicopters climbed out rapidly.

As the helicopters disappeared, and the roar from their engines faded, Tynan was up and moving again. He jumped over the rice paddy dike and fought his way toward the jungle. He reached the edge of it and stopped, checking to the left where the rest of the men were strung out.

Jacobs glanced at him and then pushed his way into the thick vegetation. Tynan followed him, moving to his left to close the line. Entering the jungle was almost like entering a steam bath. A wall of humidity rolled over him and sweat popped out on his face and body. He could feel it dripping before he had moved more than ten meters.

He caught Jacobs at the base of a mammoth teak tree. The huge, smooth trunk was nearly twenty feet in diameter. Jacobs was crouched there, one knee on the ground. He had his compass out and was checking it against the map he carried.

The men fanned out into a loose circle, facing outward, watching for signs of the enemy. Tynan glanced at the map and then at Jacobs. The big man wasn't sweating. In fact, he looked almost comfortable.

"Need to head off in that direction," he said.

Tynan nodded, but was reluctant to move. All morning, he had been waiting. First for the helicopters and then to find the LZ. He had gotten into a relaxed mode. Now, suddenly, he had to rely on all his senses. He had to be careful not to make noise, and not to trip any booby traps. Suddenly the world around him was a dangerous, hostile place, not like the relative safety in the rear of the helo.

He glanced at his watch and then nodded. They needed to get ten clicks or more from the landing site before dusk. They needed time to recon the AO so that they didn't walk into an enemy ambush.

He nodded and Jacobs got up, moving deeper into the jungle. Tynan followed and the rest of the men followed suit. They spread out so that each man could only see one other. They all moved silently, even the Army lieutenant who hadn't spent that much time in the jungle or in the training.

It wasn't a dense jungle. There was a canopy over them but the sunlight managed to get through it. Part of the ground seemed to be glowing green in the sunlight. The color was so deep and bright that it nearly hurt the eyes to look at it.

Jacobs moved them quickly, finding the path of least resistance through the jungle. Tynan tried to do nothing to disturb the ground or the plants. He didn't want some sharp-eyed VC to spot a broken branch or flattened grass or kicked-up dirt and know that someone had been near. He wanted them all to glide through the jungle like a light breeze. No one should be able to see that they had been there.

After an hour, Jacobs came to a clearing. Not much of a clearing—a single bomb crater thirty or forty feet across. The earth was matted down and there was a hint of green on the top suggesting that the crater was an old one. In the bottom was a pool of clear water.

"We rest here, Skipper?"

The thought of scrambling down the side of the crater to splash a little water on his face and the back of his neck was tempting, but he knew that Charlie would know the same thing. Charlie might not be around now, but he would know where the crater was and would probably swing by it. It would be too easy to leave signs the enemy could read.

"No. Skirt this and move deeper into the jungle. Another thirty minutes and then we rest."

"Aye aye."

They started off again, around the edge of the crater. They moved deeper into the jungle, where the canopy was thicker, cutting off the sun. Now everything was a dark green, or charcoal, or completely black. There was the noise of animals running through the undergrowth near them, birds in the sky and monkeys in the trees calling to one another.

They kept at it, moving farther to the west, toward the Cambodian border. In the east was the boom of artillery and the roar of jet engines as Air Force pilots searched for the Vietcong. Everything was happening in South Vietnam, nowhere near them.

Tynan finally called a halt, telling the men to rest, eat lunch, but to stay alert. They'd rest for an hour and then begin moving again, heading for the Cambodian border and the suspected location of the COSVN.

When they stopped, Jones moved closer and asked, "You think we'll find it?"

Tynan grinned and said, "I hope to hell not."

5

Sinclair had thought he would be dead by sunrise. The men who had charged into the trees with him were all dead. He hadn't seen their bodies, but he was convinced they had all died, either killed in the fighting after they entered the jungle, or executed shortly after capture. The Vietcong had a habit of doing that. It was easier to deal with prisoners when they were dead.

Of course, Sinclair had told his own soldiers that dead men could provide no intelligence; they couldn't help defeat the enemy because they were just dead. Charlie didn't believe in that philosophy. Charlie figured one more dead American was one fewer to fight.

For the first few seconds, after he'd felt the barrel of the AK-47 against the back of his skull, he was sure that he was going to die, too. A quick pull of the trigger, a white-hot flash of pain, and it would be all over for him. But the trigger wasn't pulled. There was a whispered conference among the Vietnamese. Sinclair was stripped of his equipment, his weapons, his ammunition, his flak jacket, and his helmet. Then he was jerked to his feet.

A single face loomed out of the darkness in front of him. Smaller and darker than Sinclair, the man stood there, his hands on his hips. He didn't say a word to Sinclair. He just stood there staring, as if he hated Sinclair with a burning desire to see him dead.

Someone jerked Sinclair's arms behind him and bound them at the elbows to restrict the use of his hands. He had to stand with his shoulders back and his spine stiff, but he could walk and maintain his balance.

No one gave him any instructions. Someone pushed him in one direction and he stumbled forward. When he stopped, he was pushed again, and this time he didn't quit moving. He fell in behind one of the enemy soldiers, following him.

They walked along a trail, one that was ill defined, almost nonexistent. There were broad-leaved plants hanging down, vines from the trees, roots sticking up through the ground, ferns off to one side and palms on the other. Animals ran through the undergrowth, making a little noise. Insects buzzed and nocturnal birds trilled.

Sinclair was baffled as he followed his Vietcong captors. He had been sure they would execute him, but that didn't happen. They said nothing to him. They walked along the jungle trail, at ease with their surroundings, some of them smoking, some of them talking in low tones. They seemed to be unconcerned with the possibility of ambush. It could mean that they had crossed the border into Cambodia, where they wouldn't expect the Americans to be. Cambodia was a sanctuary for the Vietcong and the North Vietnamese. An imaginary line on the ground that was as inviolate as the Berlin Wall. The enemy could cross with impunity, but the Americans and their allies were prohibited from crossing. No one in South Vietnam wanted to violate the neutrality of Cambodia.

The patrol slowed and then stopped for a moment, but no one cleared the trail. They stood there talking, a single man watching to make sure Sinclair didn't try to escape.

Sinclair knelt then, one knee on the soft, spongy ground. Sweat dripped from his face and his uniform was soaked. Not all of it was from the heat and humidity in the predawn jungle. He was nervous and his bladder was again full. He had to piss but didn't want to tell the Vietcong about it. Somehow, admitting to them that he was a victim of the same bodily functions as they was akin to admitting that he was inferior to them. He couldn't explain it.

In the distance, from the direction they had come, was a boom of artillery. A fire-support base firing harassment into a preselected site. The hope wasn't that they would catch the enemy in the barrage; rather, the mere fact that the Americans would intermittently drop artillery in the area might discourage movement by the enemy.

A moment later they were up and moving again. No one said anything to him. When they formed on the trail, he joined them, and when they started to move, he stepped off too.

Escape, according to the instructors at the various schools and training centers, was something that had to be accomplished as soon after capture as possible. The longer you waited, the worse the chances of success. The enemy moved you from your own lines, failed to feed you so that you were weakened, and soon moved you to a location where the whole task of the soldiers was to make sure that escape didn't happen. Simply put, the sooner, the better.

But the opportunity didn't come. There were too many of the enemy around him, watching him too closely as they worked their way through the darkened jungle. Sinclair was aware that it was getting close to morning, when he wouldn't have the cover of darkness to help him.

Again the enemy stopped, falling out along the trail. A clump of Vietcong, their weapons stacked, was seated facing east as if trying to see the war going on there. In the distance, through gaps in the light jungle growth, they could see flares hanging in the sky over some American camp. It was like a beacon for Sinclair; a lighthouse that showed him where friendly forces waited.

He turned and looked down into the grinning face of a Vietcong soldier who held an AK-47, the folded bayonet extended as if waiting for the opportunity to stick Sinclair.

"I need to piss," said Sinclair.

The man's smile widened, but he said nothing to indicate he understood a word of what Sinclair was saying.

"Come on," he said. He turned, lifting his arms to show the enemy the rope that held his elbows behind him. "I've got to piss."

Sinclair glanced over his shoulder, but the man hadn't moved. "Come on," he demanded.

Another Vietcong soldier approached and said, "You be quiet now."

Sinclair faced the new man and said, "I just wanted to take a piss. That's all."

"You wait."

"Come on, man, I'm not asking for anything much. Just a chance to take a piss."

The man stood there, staring up at Sinclair. He didn't move and didn't blink.

"Only two minutes," said Sinclair. He turned around so that the VC could get at the rope binding him.

It didn't seem that the enemy soldier was interested in Sinclair's discomfort, but then he felt a tug at the ropes. They loosened and dropped away.

"Thanks," said Sinclair. He moved to the right, off the trail. He stopped near a big teak tree and began fumbling with his fly, grinning at the man who stood watching. Sinclair slipped to the right, to the rear of the tree, and as soon as he lost sight of the VC, he whirled and ran. He leaped a single low bush, slipped and slid down the bank of a stream. He landed in it feet first with a quiet splash, but then was up and moving, grabbing at the roots and vines to haul himself up.

There was shouting behind him. Raised voices calling in Vietnamese. A single shot was fired but he didn't hear the bullet. Instead he dodged to the right, down a path, running. He couldn't see well in the dark. A tree loomed in front of him and he jumped to the left, missing it. He turned again, trying to head east. East to South Vietnam.

He stumbled, falling to his hands and knees. Rotting vegetation covered him. It smelled of mildew and death. He got up, glanced to the rear, and then ran again. His hands were out in front of him, like a blind man feeling the way, but he was running. Dodging and leaping, trying to lose the Vietnamese.

Somehow they stayed close to him. The voices spread out as they searched for him.

"Too much noise," he told himself. "Quiet."

He slowed, trying to control his breathing, his feet, the jungle. He slowed, listening to the sounds around him. Animals and insects and birds. Artillery crashed and Sinclair turned toward it, figuring that would lead him to South Vietnam.

As he hurried to the east, his head turning right and left, he listened for the enemy. Now they were quiet. No shouting. No firing. They were stalking him as a tiger would stalk its prey. Silently. Using its deadly energy to conceal itself in the darkness of the jungle.

For the moment, the advantage was Sinclair's. He could hurry forward. He knew where he was. The Vietcong had to search for him, had to move as silently as possible to have a chance of catching him.

Sinclair stopped to rest. He moved toward the trunk of a huge palm and crouched next to it, using its size to hide himself. He listened, but there was no sound from the enemy soldiers. They were out there, he knew it. They wouldn't let him get away that easily.

Glancing up to the east, he saw the first pale signs that it was near dawn. Nothing more than a hint of gray-pink and a fading of the dimmer stars. Time was now on the side of the enemy. Sinclair knew that he should find a place to hide for the day. Let the enemy expend his energy as the jungle heated and sapped strength. He could rest through the day and then move with sunset, using the darkness to conceal his movement. It was the same plan he had used the day before.

Trying to dodge the sweep he knew they were

making, he turned to the south, now walking rapidly. He was listening for sounds of the pursuit. The enemy seemed to have lost him.

Sinclair stopped again and crouched. He wiped his face and rubbed the sweat on the leg of his fatigues. It had been so simple. He'd conned them so easily. Of course, he still had to piss. With no one around him, he moved to the closest tree and finished opening his fly. Carefully, trying to make no sound, he began. It was a slow, almost painful process as he tried to control the flow so that there was no noise.

Finished, he fastened his fly and moved off again. The jungle was beginning to stir around him. Monkeys, birds, and animals were waking. Some screamed at one another, the sound of their voices covering the noise he might make. But then, it also hid the sounds of his pursuers.

Sinclair now moved cautiously, searching for a place to hide for the day. Somewhere near water so that he could get a drink before lying low. He'd need water before the day was out. The heat could sap the moisture from a stone and to be without water for the day would be the next thing to committing suicide.

Sinclair came to another small stream. He carefully made his way down the bank, holding on to the thin trunks of saplings or vines. When he reached the water, he stopped and hesitated. Then he crouched and lowered his lips, drinking deeply.

Throughout his training, throughout his tour in Vietnam, he had been warned against drinking the water without treating it. Clear water contained bacteria that caused a dozen different diseases. There were no sewage treatment plants and the people didn't understand sanitation. That didn't matter when you were lost in the jungle without food or water, having escaped from the Vietcong. You needed water and it didn't matter that it might be tainted.

Sinclair stuck his face in it, letting it wash away the sweat, and then lifted himself so that only his lips touched the surface. He sucked it in, swallowing rapidly, feeling it flow down into his belly. He kept drinking until it seemed that his stomach was bloated.

Satisfied, he pushed himself back on his knees and felt the mud of the bank slipping under him. Glancing up, he saw that the stars were fading rapidly and the sky was now gray. The tops of the jungle trees were becoming visible. In minutes the jungle would begin to brighten. He had to find a place to hide.

He stood and climbed back up to the trail he had been following. There was no one to be seen in either direction. Sinclair crossed it, pushing his way into the thicker vegetation of the jungle there. Now he had to be careful to conceal his trail. The slightest disturbance to the vegetation would point him out to the enemy.

He worked his way among the ferns dripping water, around the bushes, stepping carefully so that he didn't scuff the carpeting of rotting plants. He listened to the jungle awakening around him: noise from the animals that concealed the noise he might be making.

As he slipped around one tree, he froze. Movement to the right caught his attention. Slowly he turned his head and found himself staring down the barrel of an AK-47. He raised his hands, palms outward.

"So, you need piss," said the Vietnamese soldier.

"Yes. I have completed that function now."

"Then you ready to go?"

"If it's all the same to you," said Sinclair, "I'll just head on back to my camp."

The enemy motioned with the barrel of his weapon and Sinclair moved toward him. Now that the man was alert, Sinclair doubted he would have the opportunity to escape again. Not with the sun up and the jungle bright. And not with the rest of the Vietcong now ready for him.

They rejoined the others and waited as the search parties returned slowly. Those in camp ate a cold breakfast of fish heads and rice cakes but nothing was offered to Sinclair. Although he knew that he would need something to eat so that he could keep up his strength, he didn't ask for food. He didn't want the enemy to know that he was hungry, and he didn't want to give them the psychological advantage of their granting his request. They gave him some water without his having to ask for it, but there were always two men watching him, both outside the range of his hands. They were taking no chances.

When the whole patrol was rejoined and each of the men had eaten, they started moving again. Normally the VC hid during the day, or confined themselves to the deepest of the jungles where it would be impossible for the pilots in helicopters or jets to see them. But that wasn't the case today. They moved along trails that were well worn. Sinclair could see that many sandals had passed over the trail.

They pushed on, never concerned about being seen or walking into an ambush. As they had done the night before, the men bunched up and talked to one another in low tones. Given all that, Sinclair was convinced that he was in Cambodia and that each step being taken was moving him that much farther from South Vietnam. And each step was making it that much harder for him to escape.

He kept his eyes open for a chance, but as morning eroded into afternoon, there were no chances. The enemy had assigned two guards to watch him, neither of them dumb enough to let Sinclair get too close to them. Neither wanted him to take their weapon, or for him to get away as he had the night before. He was going to stay their prisoner this time.

At noon they stopped to eat a cold lunch of rice taken from plastic bags each man carried. Just a handful of the clumped-together rice that didn't look all that appetizing. Again no one offered Sinclair anything, but they did give him some water. After lunch, they rested with half the men sleeping in the shade of ferns and bushes and trees while the other half watched Sinclair. Since it was obvious that he wasn't going to get away from them, he found a good spot and lay down. Almost before he could get comfortable, he was asleep. It would be rest that he might need if he got the chance to run.

6

Tynan and his men never knew when they crossed the border into Cambodia. There were no walls or fences or guard towers or shacks. The border was devoid of human life. It was jungle and swamp and rice field. The terrain in Cambodia was the same as that in Vietnam. The only way Tynan knew that they had crossed was by using his map and comparing the landmarks on it with what he could see in the country around him. That convinced him that he and his men were into Cambodia.

Knowing that the North Vietnamese and the Vietcong maintained camps within ten or twenty clicks of the border, the perfect place from which to raid South Vietnam, he cautioned his men. The enemy would be all around them. Now it was time to begin moving with care, maintaining noise discipline. The only good thing was that they would no longer have to worry about booby traps. Since the enemy didn't expect Americans in Cambodia, they would booby-trap nothing.

By midday, Tynan had found the perfect place to set up his camp. They had walked up to a slight hill. Near the base, on the north side was a small, clear stream that could provide them with water. The gently sloping sides were twenty to thirty feet higher than the surrounding territory and gave Tynan a view of the jungle around him. A few men at the top could hold off a sizable force of enemy soldiers, if that enemy located them and tried to attack them. The vegetation on the slopes was spare enough to give them good killing fields while that on top was thick enough to protect them from the enemy. It was such a perfect spot that Tynan couldn't understand why the enemy didn't have a camp there already.

They moved up the slope slowly, on line, each man ready for the trap to spring, but that didn't happen. Instead, they reached the top and found themselves alone.

Tynan moved over to Jacobs and said, "Take two men and scout the north side. Look for signs of enemy activity."

"Aye aye, sir."

Jacobs took Hernandez and Wentworth and slipped into the jungle. Tynan watched them as they began their descent but then the men seemed to blend into the jungle and vanish. He grinned at the sight. It was exactly how jungle fighters should act: they should become part of the jungle, vanishing into it.

Tynan found Jones and asked, "How's the radio?"

Jones, who was crouched at the foot of a giant teak tree, said, "I could run the antenna up here so that we can maintain radio contact with our base."

"But?" said Tynan.

"But it would be better to run the antenna out about half a click. That way, if the enemy triangulates, they'll get the wrong location. Get the antenna but not the radio."

"That practical?"

"Shit, sir, the Green Berets do it all the time. Just takes a little patience and some intelligence."

"Then do it."

"Aye aye."

Tynan then found Boyson sitting on the ground, his back against a palm tree. He had taken off his helmet and set it down beside him. His face was pale and covered with sweat. His mouth hung open so that he looked as if he had died and his muscles had all relaxed.

"You okay?" asked Tynan.

Boyson looked up but seemed too tired to move. "Fine. I'm fine. You people move like this all the time?"

Tynan grinned. "Hell, we hardly worked up a good sweat."

"What's the plan?" asked Boyson, his voice weak.

"We'll stay here, set up camp, and then move out, searching for the enemy."

Boyson lifted one hand and wiped the sweat from his face. He looked at his wet fingers and then wiped them on his fatigue shirt. "There any chance we'll find out what happened to my boys?"

Tynan crouched near the other officer and took out his map. "Exactly where were you hit?"

Boyson took the map, turned it, refolded it, and pointed to a spot just south of Angel's Wing and north of Parrot's Beak. "In here. Near this area that opens toward swamp and rice paddies."

"That's what? Ten, twelve clicks from here? Doubt

that we'll range that far out until we move the camp. If we even move the camp."

"I'd appreciate the opportunity to lead some of the men in that direction."

Tynan shook his head. "Can't do it. Our mission is specific and it's not to go in search of your men."

Boyson looked up at Tynan. "Didn't you ever make a mistake that needed correcting? Didn't you ever wish you had the chance to do something over again and do it right?"

"Many times," said Tynan.

"Well, this is my chance. I did it wrong the first time, then got out before we really searched for the missing men. Now I have a chance to go look for them . . ."

"I'm sorry," said Tynan, "but we don't have the time to let you search for your men. We've got a week to find what we have to find and get out. Maybe we'll learn something in that week, but we can't go chasing after your lost men. That's not why we're here."

"Sure," said Boyson. He took his canteen from his belt and opened it. He drank, then poured some water into his cupped palm to rub the back of his neck.

"You'll find," said Tynan, "that you shouldn't waste water that way."

"We do it in the field to cool ourselves."

"Right," agreed Tynan, "but you and your men are always a helo ride from your camp. Supplies and water are within an hour of you. But not here. We've got to rely on what we have to sustain us for a week without getting in helos."

"But there's water at the base of the hill," protested Boyson.

Tynan just shook his head. There was no way to

convince the man that waste in the jungle was waste and it didn't matter where you were. He hadn't been around long enough to learn some of the brutal lessons of the jungle. He'd learned only that the enemy was brutal.

"Have it your way," said Tynan.

Cummings came up then. "Got a few trip flares spread and put out a couple of the claymores, two of them on trip wires, but I haven't hooked them up. I'll want to show Jacobs and the others where they are."

"Good," said Tynan.

"Found kind of a natural cave," added Cummings. "Small, no more than four feet deep, and maybe five, six feet across. We can use it to store our supplies and ammo, and with very little work it'll be hidden."

"Very good."

Cummings looked at his watch. "About six hours of light left. I could take Jones out on a sweep to the west."

"No," said Tynan. "We've got half our force in the field now. Let's just hang loose. You might want to watch the west side of the perimeter, though."

"Certainly."

As Cummings left, Boyson asked, "Just how are you going to run this?"

"Mainly by ear until we learn a little bit more about the terrain around us. That's the thing that can kill you as quickly as anything. You've got to know what's around you before you start making big plans."

"So we wait."

"For now," agreed Tynan.

Jacobs and his small patrol hadn't moved very far when they ran into the first signs that the Vietcong and the NVA were around. They crossed one trail that showed signs of recent use. There were footprints made from sandals cut from the tires of trucks. Jacobs halted them long enough to look down the trail and then they crossed it, moving into the jungle on the north side of it. He then turned along it, paralleling it as they searched for the enemy.

The tiny patrol strung out, moving slowly, each man trying to make no noise. They stepped in one another's footprints, moving aside the branches of bushes and ferns carefully. Jacobs, his M16 clutched in his left hand, led the way. He ignored the heat of the jungle, the insects that buzzed around his face, the animals that scampered through the trees over them. If the noise made by those animals and insects suddenly faded, then he would wonder.

For nearly an hour they moved along the edge of the trail, keeping it in sight through gaps in the foliage, searching for a living enemy on it. Just as he was about ready to turn back, he thought he heard the quiet babble of voices. He motioned Wentworth and Hernandez to wait and moved forward alone.

They had come to the edge of a large clearing. The jungle faded into a series of stages that finally gave way to the clearing. In the middle of it were three NVA soldiers. Jacobs knew they were NVA because they wore khaki uniforms and not black pajamas. Each was armed with an AK and one of them had a pistol, meaning that he was probably an officer.

For a moment, Jacobs stayed where he was, watching the enemy soldiers. It would be so easy to kill them. With the M16 on full auto, he'd be able to get them all before they had a chance to react. But then, someone was sure to hear the firing and someone else would find the bodies. That would mean that the enemy would be alerted.

Instead, Jacobs watched them. It was obvious that they didn't fear American air power. They were in the open and one of them was building a fire. In South Vietnam, such an act would bring instant death from the sky. A fighter or a helicopter would spot the smoke, investigate, and then attack. But here, on the Cambodian side of the border, the enemy could move with impunity. He was as safe, maybe safer, than he would be at home in North Vietnam.

A few minutes later, four more men joined the first three, and then four others, making eleven. They fanned out, picked up wood, and returned to the fire to throw it on. They pulled a pot over, filled it with water from their canteens, and then began throwing rice and fish into the kettle. They made no attempt to establish a perimeter, to set pickets, or put out guards. They looked like Boy Scouts in the local woods.

No one else joined them. Jacobs retreated then, moving back slowly so that he didn't make any noise or call attention to himself. Let the soldiers enjoy their hot meal. No reason for Jacobs to try to stop it.

He found both Wentworth and Hernandez where he'd left them. No one spoke. He pointed in the direction they had come and then walked past them, moving into the jungle. Now he ranged farther to the north, away from the trail. Neither of the other men asked a question. They knew that he would tell them all that they needed to know when the time came.

They hadn't moved more than half a click, maybe less, when there was more noise: a single voice speaking quietly, and then a ripple of laughter. Jacobs held up a hand to stop them. Both men peeled off, moved perpendicular to the trail a few yards, and stopped, waiting.

Again Jacobs started forward, thinking that Tynan and Walker had been right. Something was going on in the jungle around them. Lots of enemy soldiers moving about. Then, a flash of movement caught his attention and he froze. One of the soldiers was coming straight at him. Jacobs couldn't leap to either side because the movement would betray his presence. In the jungle, it was possible to hide in full view of the enemy, as long as you didn't move suddenly.

With his right hand, he touched the hilt of the knife taped upside down to the left side of his harness. Carefully, so that he didn't make a sound, he unsnapped it and felt the knife slide into his fingers. He stopped the movement and kept his eyes on the Vietcong, a young man in black pajamas, a khaki pith helmet, and a chest pouch for the three spare magazines for his AK. He seemed unaware that there was anyone in the jungle with him.

He walked right up to Jacobs without batting an eye. He kept his attention on the jungle floor, as if afraid he was going to step on something horrible there, and he walked right into Jacobs.

The big man reacted immediately. He dropped his own weapon and drew his knife in a single, fluid motion. He spun the startled man, and struck with the knife, cutting the throat. The VC coughed violently and jerked away. His hands flew to his injured neck and he squeezed, trying to stop the bleeding. He dropped to his knees and then toppled forward.

Jacobs, his eyes on the enemy soldier, who spasmed and died, retrieved his weapon. Then, for good measure, he stole the AK from the dead man. He was about to back off and then crouched over the dead man. He rolled him over, under the spreading branches of a large bush. Anyone following him might not see the body right away. In a couple of days, if the scavengers didn't get at it, the enemy would be able to find it easily.

As the flies began to gather, their frustrated buzzing getting louder, Jacobs retreated. He stopped between Hernandez and Wentworth and whispered, "I had to take one out."

"Well, shit," said Wentworth.

"Hernandez, take point. Back the way we came. I'll guard the rear. No noise."

"Right."

They moved off then, back to the camp, but avoided using their original line of march. Even though the enemy in Cambodia wasn't as alert as their counterparts in South Vietnam, it didn't mean that they were completely incompetent. Using the same path was one of the quickest ways to get killed. Hernandez led them north, away from the trail they had paralleled, and then turned to the south, moving toward the hill where the camp was hidden.

Going back seemed easier than going out. Maybe it was because they had a destination and they had seen some of the terrain as they had walked through the jungle. They knew where they were going and what to expect.

As they approached the hill, they slowed, advancing up it carefully so that the men there would have a chance to identify them. They reached the crest, but could find no signs that the others were there. Tynan appeared then and pointed at the others. They had effectively concealed themselves and their camp so that the enemy wouldn't be able to stumble on it.

It was a simple thing to do. Live in the jungle as a part of it and not worry about the things campers in the World did. Instead of cutting down saplings, lashing them together, and then covering the mess with broad leaves cut from some of the nearby trees, they strung their field hammocks so that they got some protection from the rain by using the natural cover of the trees and bushes. They didn't walk across the center of the hill, but around the sides, making sure that they didn't crush the small plants or scuff the jungle floor. They kept movement to a minimum.

Jacobs found the lieutenant near the trunk of a huge tree. From this vantage point, he could see out onto a sea of green that stretched from the hill to Vietnam. There was nothing to see out there. An unbroken expanse of jungle that faded into the distance. No movement, no smoke, no aircraft in the sky. It looked as if they had set down on a planet where there was no animal life. Just the thick jungle vegetation that had no competition from the animal kingdom.

"Ran into a patrol that seemed to be on a picnic," whispered Jacobs. He then described everything that he had seen and told Tynan that he'd had to kill a man.

"Wished you hadn't done that," said the lieutenant.

"So do I," responded Jacobs, "but there was nothing I could do about it. He walked right up to me. Looked me right in the face."

"You hide the body?" asked Tynan.

"Best I could, but hell, after a day or so, anyone with a nose is going to be able to find it."

"Still," said Tynan, "the attitude is going to be that we don't operate in Cambodia so that even if they find him, they probably won't begin looking too hard for us."

"Anything else, Skipper?"

"That's about got it."

Tynan nodded and turned his attention back to the open area that he could see through the gap in the trees. Quietly he said, "Let's get some rest and start the search in the morning."

"Aye aye, sir," said Jacobs. He moved off to find a spot to put his hammock.

7

Tynan and his men were up with the sun. Before the cacophony of noise from the monkeys and birds had died, they were ready to begin the first full day of patrolling. After a cold breakfast of field rations made from dried beef rather than the canned C-ration meals favored by the Army, they broke up into three small teams. Two to patrol and one to remain behind to hold the camp.

Tynan, working with Jacobs, moved off to the east with an eye to the south. Hernandez, working with Jones, moved directly south and then would bend around to the east before returning. They would use the morning to fan out and the afternoon to return, arriving at the camp an hour or so before dark, if everything went the way it was supposed to.

Without saying much to the men, Tynan began to slip away into the jungle. Communications, if needed, would be by URC-10, a small, hand-held ultrahigh frequency radio that had a range of over a hundred miles. He could maintain radio communications with either the base or the other men in the field, if that became necessary.

With Jacobs five or six yards behind him, he moved down the hillside into the depths of the jungle. He moved slowly, taking it easy, making sure to leave no sign for the enemy. He slipped along, avoiding the game trails and farmers' paths because the enemy could be using them and that could lead to a fight. The game trails were something else again. The jungle cats, notably the tigers, sometimes lay in ambush along them, waiting for their lunch. Others were used by elephants. Those were obvious by the huge piles steaming on the jungle floor.

Instead, they worked their way through the vegetation, looking and listening. They hadn't gotten very far, had avoided disturbing a flock of birds in the trees, and then heard the sound of voices. Tynan held up a hand and then pointed to the ground near where he stood, telling Jacobs to take that position and then to hold.

When Jacobs was in position, Tynan moved forward slowly, carefully. As he neared the location of the Vietnamese voices, he got down on his hands and knees and then stretched out on his stomach. He listened closely, but the words were lost in the quiet rustling of the leaves on the light breeze. He crept forward then, moving one hand and then one foot, being careful not to disturb the vegetation.

He stopped once, his forehead resting on his hand. He could smell the jungle floor—a rotting stench that filled his nostrils and his mouth. He could feel the sweat on his body, too. It dripped from his face and ran down his back and sides to soak his uniform, turning it black. He was hot, the humidity trapped under the triple canopy of the jungle.

He started forward again, using the sound of the voices to guide him. He pushed past a huge tree, slipped over the roots sticking up through the dirt and rotting vegetation of the jungle, and then stopped.

Through the lacy branches of a giant fern, he could see an area that opened up, almost like a park in the World. The ground had been cleared of plants, bushes, ferns, vines, and saplings. Only the largest of the trees remained, looking like huge brown pillars supporting a curved ceiling that had been painted a deep, rich green. The illusion was of an auditorium that would hold a thousand or more.

The illusion didn't stop there. Facing him, a hundred meters away, was a set of bleachers that were loaded with enemy soldiers. Dressed in the khaki of the NVA and the black pajamas of the VC, each holding a weapon, from the SKS to the AK and from captured M1 carbines to the newest of the M16s, dozens of them sat looking down at a single man standing beside a sheet-covered easel.

For all the world, it looked like a briefing session prior to an exercise back in the States. One man telling the participants what was expected of them and giving them an overview of the upcoming events. There didn't seem to be anything sinister or hostile about it. Just an outdoors briefing for the men.

Tynan studied it carefully, wishing there were a way to call in an air strike or artillery. Such a strike would kill most of the men and destroy the camp, if it was handled right. It would be a blow to the enemy's morale, telling him that the Americans could reach out and swat him no matter how safe he thought he was.

But that wouldn't happen. He'd have to give coordinates and those coordinates would show that he was inside Cambodia. Even if he could get permission to fire, that permission would probably have to come from MACV Headquarters in Saigon and it would be a couple hours before it could be secured. By then, the enemy would be gone so that if the permission was given, the artillery would fall on empty ground.

Studying the area around the bleachers, Tynan noticed that there was a ring of bunkers. Not the deeply dug, almost completely hidden things used in South Vietnam, but shallow bunkers made of log and dirt, sitting on the ground. It was one more indication that the Vietcong and the North Vietnamese didn't expect to be attacked in Cambodia.

Satisfied that he had seen everything he could, Tynan began creeping to the rear, still watching the enemy's class. He rejoined Jacobs and the two of them detoured to the south, avoiding the enemy classroom.

They hadn't gone far when they came to another enemy camp. This one was made of thatched hootches set in four rows and protected from sight by the thick jungle overhead. There was a fence around it, six feet high and made of barbed wire. Guard towers, no more than six feet tall, were scattered along the fence but seemed to be unmanned. Near the center of the camp was a larger, concrete blockhouse that blossomed with antenna. A radio shack of some kind.

Jacobs crawled close to Tynan and put his lips next to the lieutenant's ear. "Think maybe we've found the COSVN already?"

Tynan studied the camp and then shook his head.

"I don't think there is a COSVN. I think it's scattered all over the place."

"Which means?"

"It means that we're right in the center of the COSVN, but there isn't one small camp, one building where everything is housed. It's a decentralized command structure."

Hernandez led Jones off the hill into a valley that somehow seemed wetter and hotter than anywhere else in the Cambodian jungle. Water dripped from the trees and the bushes, and the ground under their feet was soft. The footprints filled with water quickly until the slowly expanding carpet filled them, making them invisible again. There was a hiss from the jungle, as if the water was boiling away, and there were patches of fog that somehow looked more like steam. There was nothing cool or refreshing about the jungle.

They walked through it slowly, each of them feeling as if he had been wrapped in a warm, wet towel. The sweat bathed them, soaking their uniforms, threatening to rot them in hours. The moisture got into everything, trying to rust it if it couldn't rot it.

In less than a click, both men were worn down. Both longed for water but both refused to take it. The danger in the jungle was dehydration, which was strange with so much water around them. Hernandez kept the pace slow, listening for sounds that the enemy was near them.

Before long, they came to the first indication that someone else was alive in the jungle. Hernandez waved Jones to cover and then got down himself. They waited as the voices became louder. Hernandez waved a hand at Jones, who burrowed under a bush so that it was nearly impossible to see him.

The enemy appeared then, moving east to west. There was a single man, dressed in khaki and carrying an AK-47. He wore a chest pouch for his spare magazines, had a round canteen, and wore a pistol belt. On his head was a pith helmet with a single red star in the center of it. He carried his weapon by the barrel, the butt of it on his shoulder. He didn't look like a soldier on patrol, but more like a hunter on a stroll in the forest.

There were two men behind him and then a cluster: men dressed in both black pajamas and khakis. And in the center of that group was one man dressed in jungle fatigues. Hernandez couldn't move then, afraid that he would alert the enemy, but he tried to confirm what he saw: a single American soldier in jungle fatigues, surrounded and watched by the enemy.

When they were past him, Hernandez crawled to the rear where Jones hid. He asked, his voice low, almost impossible to hear, "You see that?"

Jones nodded.

"I want to follow, see if we can find out where they're going."

Again Jones nodded and then whispered, "I'm right behind you."

Hernandez waited until the rear guard, three men walking together smoking cigarettes and joking quietly, passed. They seemed not to have a care in the world. Once they were out of sight Hernandez moved to the trail, glanced down it, and then crossed it, Jones right behind him.

Together they paralleled the trail, staying in the trees and using the bushes for cover. They could hear the enemy in front of them, talking and laughing.

They could stay close by, listening to the soldiers.

Thirty minutes later, the enemy stopped. Hernandez moved forward slowly, crawling on the ground so that the enemy wouldn't see him. He managed to get within fifteen feet of the enemy and studied their camp. They all sat around in a circle, drinking from their canteens and smoking cigarettes. No one seemed to be on guard except for one man who was watching the lone American. Hernandez could see that he was a captured soldier now.

He withdrew and said to Jones, "There's too many of them for us to take them."

"They get to camp, it's not going to get any easier."

Hernandez shook his head. "That's not true. In the dark we can sneak in and free the man. Might find a few others in the bargain."

Jones had nothing to say to that. He just stared off into the jungle and waited.

The Vietcong and NVA began to move again. They broke their camp, and continued on to the west. Hernandez and Jones followed along, staying well back and listening to the noise the enemy was making.

They tracked them through the morning, waited while they ate a cold lunch, and then started off again. Hernandez knew they were going to have to break off soon if they planned to reach the camp before nightfall, but he didn't want to lose sight of the prisoner. Freeing the man would be a big morale boost to everyone fighting in South Vietnam. Very few of the men captured managed to escape.

Just as he thought they were going to have to break return to camp, the enemy stopped again. They spread out into the trees and then, suddenly, the man in the center disappeared. Hernandez lay there trying to figure it out when the enemy popped up again. The VC had come to an underground entrance, or possibly to a tunnel complex.

"They'll stay the night here," said Jones quietly.

Hernandez nodded slowly. If it was a way station, a kind of safe house, they wouldn't be inclined to leave it during the night. That would mean that they would be there in the morning. It was time to get out.

Quietly, they withdrew, crawling to the rear. When they were far enough away that they thought it was safe, they got up and began to walk. Not the quiet, calm stroll of the weekend hiker, but a slower, more careful pace. They were still intent on not making any noise or leaving any sign for the enemy.

At the hillside camp, Cummings and Wentworth spent the early hours making sure everything was hidden so that the casual observer would see nothing unusual. That done, Wentworth worked his way down to the stream and carefully washed his face and hair. Not that it would do much good in the jungle, but the act cooled him, giving him some momentary relief from the humidity threatening them all.

Finished, he filled the canteens and carefully walked back to the crest of the hill. Once there, he put the halazone tablets into each of the canteens and set them aside to give the chemicals a chance to work.

Cummings was going to make the trek down the hill to the stream to wash when a noise on the eastern side of the hill caught his attention. He froze and slipped to the ground, stretching out on his belly. With one hand on his weapon, he crawled forward until he spotted a group of men coming up the hill toward him. It was a ragtag bunch, armed with a variety of weapons and dressed in clothes that looked stolen from all the participants in the Vietnam War. There were American jungle fatigues and Vietcong pajamas and North Vietnamese khakis. One man wore the remains of a gray flight suit that looked like those worn by Navy fliers.

The appearance of the men was no better. Long, stringy hair, beards, and mustaches. They looked as if they hadn't washed in days, maybe weeks. They didn't look like soldiers in the field, but more like Cambodian bandits. Cummings had heard that there were bandits, drug runners, who worked both sides of the Cambodian border.

Convinced that he had seen bandits, he retreated to where Wentworth was checking his weapon for dirt. Wentworth glanced up as Cummings approached, but didn't say a word.

Cummings leaned close and said, "We've company. Ten, twelve bandits coming up the hill."

Wentworth nodded and began to reassemble his rifle as fast as he could. As he slapped the magazine home, Boyson appeared and asked, "What the fuck is going on?"

Wentworth wanted to slap the shit out of him for speaking so loud, but didn't. He put one finger to his lips and then pointed to the east.

"Oh," said Boyson as he turned to look. Then he dropped to one knee and said again, "Oh."

"We've got to spread out," whispered Cummings. "No noise. Let them pass."

"Got it," said Boyson unnecessarily.

Cummings, using the available cover, moved across the plateau and then dropped to the ground using a rock and rotting log for cover.

Just as he fell from sight, the first of the men appeared on the top of the hill. He stood there, a rifle held in his hands, a cigarette in his mouth. He didn't say anything, just stood there looking around, as if he thought something might be wrong.

A moment later, two more of the men joined him. One of them grunted something, shoved the first man on the shoulder, and then laughed. The man sat down on a stone, his rifle clutched in his hands, the butt sitting on the ground between his feet.

More of the men appeared then, spreading out. They dropped to the ground. One of them pulled out his canteen and drank from it, handing it to one of his friends. They were all talking in low tones, laughing about something.

Cummings glanced to the right, where he could just see Boyson lying on the ground. The army officer was staring at the bandits. In his hand he clutched his rifle and was slowly moving it forward as if he thought he could open fire and hit all the bandits with one well-placed burst.

There was no way Cummings could stop him. Boyson was operating on another level. He thought he had something to prove and here was his chance to prove it. It made no difference that a grandstand play here might result in their getting killed. Cummings didn't understand it, but knew that the only thing he could do was support Boyson, if he did try something. Later he could say something to Boyson, if they survived. Later he could slap the shit out of Boyson—if they survived.

Boyson rolled to his right, lifting his weapon as he did. There was a quiet snap of a twig and one of the bandits turned to look. Boyson came up then, off the ground. Firing from the hip, he shot the closest bandit, who pitched to the right, blood spurting.

As the rounds slammed into the first of the bandits, the others scattered. One of them opened fire with an AK-47. Cummings spotted him and fired once. The round smashed into the man's head. He tossed his weapon up as he rolled over.

Firing broke out around them. AK-47s against M16s. There were single shots from M1s and SKSs. A rippling fire that tore into the jungle around him. Bits of bark, pieces of leaves rained down on him.

Wentworth, on the other side of the hilltop, fired a short burst and then rolled away. He fired again and then dropped down out of sight.

The bandits were shouting at one another. They were shooting at everything that moved. There were single bursts, long, drawn-out firing, and then a tapering.

Cummings crawled down the side of the hill while Wentworth and Boyson continued to put out rounds. Wentworth was firing single shot, but Boyson was on full auto, burning through his ammunition as fast as he could pull the trigger and switch magazines.

One of the bandits yelled something then, loudly. The shooting slowed and stopped. The voice of the bandit came again, speaking slowly, as if unfamiliar with the words.

Cummings didn't understand much Vietnamese. He had been in Vietnam long enough to learn a few words, but not the string that the man was shouting at him. He crept forward along the side of the hill until he spotted one of the enemy kneeling behind a bush. He was watching the shouting man.

Cummings slung his weapon and pulled out the Randall Combat Knife taped upside down to his harness. Without making a sound, he approached the man. When he was in striking distance, he snapped out his left hand, grabbed the man, and pulled to the rear. The man gasped and tried to scream, but Cummings was ready. He lifted the head and slashed at the throat. As the blood splashed, Cummings jammed the knife in, over the kidney and then up toward the lungs and heart. There was a spasm of pain and the man stiffened and then suddenly relaxed.

Cummings rolled the body away and picked up the AK the man had dropped. It was in poor shape, looking as if it had never been cleaned. He slipped back, sliding down the hill away from the enemy.

The shouting was still going on; the leader of the Cambodian bandits was trying to get someone to speak to him. Concealed behind the trees and vegetation of the jungle, Cummings couldn't see the man.

Then, suddenly, one of the Americans shouted, "Grenade!"

Cummings dropped to the ground. He heard the grenade crash through the trees and hit the ground. A second later there was an explosion. Firing broke out immediately. AKs and M16s on full auto. Cummings saw another of the bandits running through the trees. He lifted his weapon and aimed, squeezed the trigger. The round knocked the man off his feet. Cummings didn't see him after he dropped.

Now he moved down the hillside farther and began working his way to the rear. Again the shout "Grenade!" came. There was an explosion, followed by another and another. The bandit leader began screaming again. The firing tapered again.

Cummings began to move back toward the enemy's line. He saw another of the men running, cradling his right arm in his left hand. It was stained with bright red blood. The man didn't seem to be thinking. He was running in a full panic.

Cummings stood up and aimed. He fired once, saw the man tumble, catch his balance, and continue to run for another two or three steps. Then suddenly he pitched forward, sprawling among the bushes and ferns.

The firing suddenly died. There was one single shot and then complete silence. No animals were moving and no birds were calling. The last echoes of the firing were fading in the distance.

Cummings moved along the side of the hill, trying to get behind the position that had been held by the bandits. He didn't stand up, but moved forward cautiously, listening for signs that the bandits were lying in ambush for him.

He came to one body: the side of the head was a bloody mess, the bone and brain showing through; flies were already crawling into the wound.

Cummings retrieved the weapon, an old and worn SKS, lying near the outstretched hand. He slung it and continued on. The next man had been killed by a grenade. The shrapnel had shredded his chest, ripping it open and exposing his heart and lungs. His weapon, lying near him, was twisted by the force of the explosion.

As he moved around, he found Wentworth moving among the dead. He'd already collected three weapons and the chest pouches from a couple men. One looked stained with fresh bloodstains.

"We get them all?"

Cummings shrugged. "I think so. I hope so."

"Who were they?"

"I think they were bandits, members of the KKK. Lot of them in Cambodia."

"Yeah," said Wentworth, but he didn't sound too convinced of it.

Without another word, Cummings moved on. He found another two bodies, plucked the weapons and spare ammo from them. He made sure that each of the men was dead and then moved on.

He got back to the center of the hill and dropped the weapons into the stack that Wentworth had made. Then he moved off to the right to one of the tall trees and leaned against it.

"You okay?" asked Wentworth.

"Fine," said Cummings. "We're going to have to evacuate the hill now. We've lost our camp."

"We'll have to bury the bodies."

"Why? The VC find the remains they'll just think that one of their own patrols took them out."

"Still, we should get rid of the bodies."

"I think," said Cummings, "that we should get ready to move out so that when the Skipper returns, we can leave."

"Damn, he's not going to like this."

"Not our fault," said Cummings. He looked past Wentworth to where Boyson was examining the captured weapons. "Not our fault," he repeated.

8

Sinclair hadn't been given anything to eat for two days. His captors made sure he had enough water to keep going, but they didn't feed him. He wondered if they had been told not to give him food because that would reduce the chances of his escape. A hungry man, weakened by lack of food, was easier to recapture, and easier to control, than one who was well feed and well rested.

They had moved from the jungles and rice paddies of South Vietnam, across the border into Cambodia. Although he'd often complained about the sanctuary offered the enemy by the imaginary line on the ground, he had never realized just how right he had been. It was the difference between night and day.

In South Vietnam, the Vietcong and North Vietnamese moved at night, staying close to the protective cover of the jungle and the triple canopy. There was no talking. The point man was separated from the main body by ten meters or more. There were flankers and a rear guard. Noise discipline was enforced and the men were ready for a fight at any moment. They scanned the sky for American fighters and helicopters, and more than once scattered, hiding in the dense vegetation as American aircraft crossed the sky above them.

Then suddenly, the discipline fell apart. The point retreated to the main body and the men began joking and talking among themselves. They slung their weapons and stopped watching the jungle around them. Cigarettes were passed around as the rear guard caught up to them. Sinclair realized that they were no longer in South Vietnam. They were in Cambodia.

But even with the sudden decline in discipline, the enemy soldiers kept a close eye on Sinclair. He'd already tried to escape once and they weren't going to take a chance on losing their prize again.

They moved through the early morning fog that clung to the ground and the trees, making the jungle seem to be on fire. They continued to midday when the heat wrapped them and threatened to kill them. They spread out among the trees, staying out of the patchy sun and ate, drank, and slept.

But all the while, one or two of the men kept an eye on Sinclair. No opportunity to escape presented itself and he couldn't just take off running. No man could outrun a bullet and if he annoyed them too much, they were liable just to gun him down.

Through the hot afternoon, he waited for everyone to fall asleep, contemplating the best route of escape. To the west and then north because the enemy would believe he'd run to the east. But the

Vietcong never let him have the chance. There was always one man awake, watching him, his hand on a rifle, ready.

About four in the afternoon they started off again, moving through the jungle slowly, laughing and joking, but always with one or two men waiting for Sinclair to make his break. Always there were one or two men watching him closely.

Finally they walked out under an expanse of canopy that concealed them from the area. The ground around him looked like the manicured grass of a park at home, with nothing growing wild. One of the men walked to the center and disappeared. A second later he stood up, looking as if he had fallen to the waist in some kind of hole.

Sinclair was pushed forward toward the hole and although he didn't want to drop down into the earth, there was no choice. When the first man turned and disappeared, Sinclair dropped into the tunnel entrance feet first. He landed and then peered into the first of three tunnels, all about knee high. Cool air seeped from each of them and there was the odor of a freshly turned grave.

Far down the one in front of him he could see the shining face of a Vietcong soldier. Those who had escorted him to that spot stood over him, shouting down at him and pointing at the tunnel.

Figuring that there was nothing he could do, he crouched and crawled into the first tunnel. It was barely wide enough for his shoulders. He lay down on the soft, moist earth and pulled himself forward, trying to avoid hitting the sides of the tunnel. He was suddenly afraid of a cave-in.

As he crawled toward the light where the other man waited, he told himself that the tunnel

wouldn't collapse. The Vietcong had used tunnels
for years. They knew how to construct them and
even if it did collapse, they could dig him out in
minutes. The secret of survival would be to protect
his head and face and give himself some breathing
room.

But the tunnel didn't collapse. He reached the
end of it and pulled himself out onto a wide shelf.
Opposite was a ladder that disappeared down into
the ground. Now the first soldier was at that level,
shouting up at him. Sinclair climbed down the ladder, unprepared for what he found at the foot of the
hole.

As he stepped out onto the ground, the whole area
behind him opened up into a wide, high cavern.
There was a slat flooring made of wood, which allowed the water to drain through into the ground. The
walls had been hacked away so that the room was
nearly twenty feet across and fifteen to twenty feet
deep. In the walls were shelves big enough to hold a
man. Each was covered with straw, suggesting they
were used for bedding. Tiny electric lights were sus-
pended from the ceiling, and from somewhere came
the hum of a generator.

A man dressed in an ornate khaki uniform with red
patches on the collar stepped into the room and said,
"You are a prisoner of the People's Army of North
Vietnam."

That didn't seem to call for a response, so Sinclair
said nothing. He stood there, wishing that someone
would give him something to eat and drink.

"You will tell me," said the officer, "your name,
your unit, and your mission in South Vietnam."

"I am David Sinclair, Sergeant, United States
Army. My serial number is RA one six nine one

seven zero four four. My date of birth is October two seven, nineteen forty nine. And that is all I'm required to tell you."

The man grinned and said, "Sergeant, I am sure that you are tired and hungry. A little unimportant information from you and I will see that you are given food, water, and a comfortable place to rest."

"David Sinclair, Sergeant—"

"Please do not bore me with a repeat of those statistics. I already know them. I would like to know your unit and what you are doing." The enemy officer grinned then. "You might as well tell me that much. Your patch on your uniform tells me your unit."

Sinclair didn't say a word. He had been told that he was not to debate with his captors. Any response he made, other than to provide the information required by the Geneva Convention, would be considered a victory by the enemy.

The enemy officer moved closer. He stopped walking and an aide set a chair behind him. The officer sat down without looking to the rear and said, "You feel an obligation to your unit and that is understandable, but if they had not run and left you behind, you would not be here. Now, you give me the information required by the Geneva Convention as your superiors have told you to do. They tell you that it is all that you must give and that your captors must respect your rights under the convention."

Still Sinclair didn't speak. He stood almost at attention, watching the enemy officer. There was nothing he wanted to say.

"But my government didn't sign that document and we are not obligated to observe it." He grinned wider. "Your superiors probably didn't mention that fact to you."

Sinclair started to shake his head and then realized what the man was doing. Start a debate, make a statement, draw the prisoner into a conversation. The subject matter was unimportant as long as the dialog was started. Once that had been established, it was easy to draw the prisoner into other conversations. It was an old interrogation technique. Sinclair wouldn't say a word.

The officer sat there, staring up at Sinclair for nearly a minute, waiting for Sinclair to say something. When that didn't happen, the officer rose and left the area without a word to anyone. Sinclair was then pushed across the floor and into a tiny alcove carved in the wall of the cavern. An iron gate was locked in place over the entrance. He was left to think about what would happen to him in the near future. No one offered either food or drink.

While Wentworth was taking down the antenna and Boyson was pulling the hidden supplies from the small stone cavern where they were concealed, Cummings worked at clearing the perimeter of trip flares and claymore mines. The plan was to get out just as soon as Tynan and the others returned.

As they finished the task, the first of the patrols returned. Tynan, who lead Jacobs up the side of the hill, asked, "What in the hell is going on here?"

Cummings moved closer and said, "I think we ran into a band of bandits. KKK. We had to fight."

"You get them all?"

Cummings nodded. "I think so. But that shouldn't matter. They weren't VC or NVA."

"But they might contact the VC and tell them we're around," said Tynan.

"Can't see that."

Tynan ignored him. "We need to get everything picked up and get ready to move. Cummings, I want you to take a position at the base of the hill on the west and watch for the enemy. As soon as the other patrol is in, we'll get out."

Tynan crossed the top of the hill and found one of the dead men. He crouched over the body, studying it. From the ragtag uniform, the beard, and the shaggy hair, it was obvious that the man wasn't a member of either the North Vietnamese Army or the Vietcong. His facial features and skin tones suggested he was Cambodian rather than Vietnamese. Tynan had been surprised to learn that the Cambodians were distinguishable from the Vietnamese, just as the montagnards were different from the Vietnamese and Cambodians.

He left the body where he found it and moved back to his men. To Cummings, he said, "I think you're right about the identity. And you're absolutely right about having to abandon this hilltop."

Before he could say more, Hernandez burst from the jungle. He was bathed in sweat and was breathing hard. "Skipper," he rasped, "we've found a captured American."

Boyson almost leaped at Hernandez. "You see who it was? Can you tell me what he looked like?"

Hernandez looked from the Army officer to Tynan. He wiped the sweat from his face and rubbed it on the chest of his fatigue jacket. "Big man. Young. Looked like he hadn't been captured more than a couple of days ago."

"You know where they took him?" asked Tynan.

"Yeah. Followed them until they entered a tunnel complex. Figured they'd be there until morning so that we could get in and grab that guy."

Tynan stared at the NCO and then at the Army lieutenant. He shook his head and said, "Our mission was specific: locate the COSVN and do not make contact with the enemy."

"Contact has already been made," said Boyson.

"Not really," said Tynan. "Those men aren't the enemy. They're bandits, so we've managed to technically obey our orders."

Boyson's face drained of color. "You're not saying that you're not going to rescue the man, are you? We've got to do everything we can to get him out."

Tynan shook his head. "Our orders are specific."

"Skipper," said Jones.

Tynan glanced at the young man and knew what he was going to say. They had to try to rescue the prisoner even if it compromised the rest of the mission. The COSVN might be a myth created by the brass hats in Saigon to cover the failure of some of their plans, but the prisoner was a fellow American who needed their help. They were obligated to risk all in an attempt to free the man.

"How far is it to this tunnel system?"

Hernandez wiped his face again and crouched down. He pulled his map from his pocket. "I make it a couple of clicks. Terrain isn't all that rough, we could make it there before dark."

Tynan looked at the map, which showed nothing but the terrain and the jungle. No indication of buildings or villages or rice paddies. Nothing but the jungle.

"What's it look like around there?"

"Jungle. No signs of anything until you get up close. Then the jungle thins."

Tynan opened up the map. "It's four or five clicks to a camp that Jacobs and I found. There're four or five hundred VC and NVA soldiers in that camp. We get into a firefight and they could hear the shooting."

"We'd still have a four- or five-click head start. They wouldn't be able to catch us."

Tynan had to agree with that, especially if they headed south rather than east. South would keep them in Cambodia longer, but it wasn't the direction the enemy would expect them to take.

"This is a tunnel system?" Tynan asked.

"That's our assumption. Saw the whole squad disappear into it."

"We're not prepared to explore or fight in a tunnel system," said Tynan.

Hernandez rocked back on his heels. "We didn't spend a lot of time there, but there were no indications of other entrances. I don't think the complex is very big."

"But you don't know."

"Oh hell," snapped Boyson. "This is pointless. We have to go in and free the man."

Tynan turned and looked up at the Army man. "That kind of thinking could get us killed. We're not going to charge in there without learning more about the situation." He turned his attention back to Hernandez. "Any signs of heavy use there?"

"That was the thing, Skipper. Didn't seem to be much indication that the enemy used the tunnels there. Vegetation was green and healthy, didn't look worn. It'd been cut back some, but that doesn't mean much."

"How big was the squad?"

"Fairly small. No more than fifteen men altogether, armed with AKs and SKSs, and an officer with a pistol. No signs of heavier weapons. But then, in the tunnel a machine gun or a grenade launcher isn't going to do you much good."

Now Tynan rubbed his face. He stared at the map and couldn't think of a reason why they shouldn't go look. They knew there was an American being held. That was all he should have to know: an American needed help. It was almost an unwritten law. You did everything you could to assist your fellow Americans.

"All right. We move out in ten minutes. Hernandez, you have point. Jones, you've got the slack. Boyson, I don't want to hear a lot of shit from you. We'll take a look, but if it turns out that there are more enemy soldiers there than we can handle, we're going to back off."

"Yes sir," said Boyson.

Tynan handed the map back to Hernandez and found Cummings. "I want you to bring up the rear. Stay back far enough that you can get out if we should walk into something. You'll be on your own to get back to Walker and tell him that this area is loaded with VC and NVA, but we found nothing that resembles an army headquarters."

"Yes sir. What's that mean?"

"It means that I think there is no COSVN. It means that we've been chasing a phantom. I think that there might be one officer who is in command of the region, but there is not a headquarters in the sense that we have MACV in Saigon or CINCPAC in Hawaii."

"Got it, Skipper."

Tynan turned then and saw that Cummings and

Boyson were shouldering their packs. Jones had rolled up the wire he'd used for the radio antenna and was storing it in his pack. Too often the Americans had decided it wasn't worth the effort to police their campsites. An empty tin can, a broken entrenching tool, or a dropped round were not worth the effort to pick them up. All those things had a way of coming back to haunt the Americans. The round could become part of a booby trap designed to shatter a foot or break a leg. The tin can would be used in a dozen different ways, all of which weren't good for the Americans. The entrenching tool could become a weapon used in an ambush.

Hernandez approached him and asked, "What'll we do with the captured weapons?"

Tynan's first instinct was to strip the bolts from them, take out the trigger housings and the other small parts, and scatter them, but then he thought better of it. The weapons and the ammo might come in handy. "Let's take them and the spare ammo with us. Might come in handy if we decide to hit the tunnel system."

"Aye aye, sir."

A moment later, Hernandez handed him two AKs and two chest pouches for them. "These are yours, sir."

Tynan laughed. "That's what I get for deciding that. Give me the lion's share."

"No sir, just your fair share."

"We about ready?"

Hernandez turned and surveyed the hilltop. Jones was standing in the center of it holding two enemy weapons. He had the radio on his back and looked ready. Cummings and Wentworth were near him, waiting. Boyson was nervously shifting from one foot to the other, anxious to get moving, although he didn't know what they were about to step into.

"Yes sir, we're all ready."

"Then let's do it," he said. He hoped that he wasn't making a mistake that would cost him and his men their lives.

9

With Hernandez on point, moving rapidly through the jungle, they made their way back toward the location where Hernandez had seen the enemy disappear. They stayed away from the trails and paths, paralleling some, crossing others. They moved as rapidly as possible, trying to keep from making noise. They strained their ears, listening for signs that the enemy was close. The warm, muggy air was like a physical barrier they had to fight their way through. Before they had traveled far, they were soaked with sweat, but that didn't slow them. Tynan had said that he needed to see the site before dark.

And unlike their initial move into the territory, they weren't as careful as they had been. A few broken branches or footprints would not tell the enemy anything he wouldn't know shortly. Now speed was more important than the lack of sign. Hernandez kept the pace rapid, knowing that they had a deadline to meet.

He stopped once and consulted his map, checking the few landmarks visible through the trees. The bed of an intermittent stream that was now made of dusty rocks and a few stagnant pools swarming with mosquitoes. A ridge line that grew up gradually and then steeply to an outcropping that was a gray veiled in green. To the south the jungle floor dropped away until, through gaps in the vegetation, they could see a river valley in the distance.

Using his compass, Hernandez sited on a single tree with a gray trunk and then started off toward it. The patrol strung out behind him, following him. Finally he slowed and then waited for Tynan to catch up.

"We're getting close," he whispered.

Tynan surveyed the area in front of him. Not thick vegetation, but a cleared area under the high canopy. If anyone had cared, there were good killing fields all around it. There seemed to be no sign of bunkers or defensive works, but then, this was Cambodia and the VC and NVA didn't expect to have to defend it.

Tynan and Hernandez crept forward, bellies on the ground, rifles held in their hands and kept off the ground to keep the breeches clear. Using their elbows, knees, and feet, they moved forward to the very edge of the jungle. Tynan looped the sling of his rifle over his hand to keep the bolt and breach out of the dirt and used his binoculars to observe the park-like area.

Although Hernandez had told him that the trapdoor for the tunnel was in the center of it, pointing it out carefully, Tynan could see no sign of it. He swept the binoculars from one side of the area to the other, but saw nothing that looked like it hid the entrance. There could be a hundred trapdoors out there and Tynan couldn't see one of them.

"You sure this is the right place?" he asked.

"Yes sir. No doubt about it."

Tynan studied it again, this time with an eye on assaulting it. This was something that they didn't teach at the school in Coronado. In fact, no one taught it anywhere. He'd have to take the things he'd learned in a half dozen other places and apply it to what he was seeing in front of him.

As he swept the open field again, he wished he were back in Coronado in a practice field exercise. Those were simpler only because he knew going in that no one was going to get killed. Someone might get hurt, but the Navy wouldn't allow the trainees to get killed.

To Hernandez he said, "There could be a division down there."

"Yes sir. But as you can see, a large unit has not moved through here. I don't care how good the VC are, they can't move a battalion through an area without leaving some sign."

Tynan nodded his agreement. But that didn't mean that there weren't other entrances that the division or battalion could use. Maybe they had found the back door.

At that moment, Jones crawled closer and said, "Skipper, we've got someone coming up behind us."

Tynan turned and searched the jungle behind them. At first he heard and saw nothing, and then came a single voice, whispering something in Vietnamese.

"Size of the enemy unit?"

"Can't say. A squad. Maybe ten men."

Hernandez said, "We can't let them enter the tunnels. That would increase the odds against us."

"And we can't get into a firefight," countered Tynan. "That would alert the men in the tunnels."

"Sir, they're getting closer."

Tynan turned and got to his knees. He turned his binoculars to the rear, but could see nothing through them. "Where are they?"

Jones pointed toward the southeast. "Wentworth and Jacobs are moving toward them."

"Shit. They coming toward this clearing?"

"That's what we're trying to find out."

"Hernandez, you stay here and watch that tunnel entrance. All we need is to be caught between the two groups. Jones, let's go."

Moving carefully, Tynan and Jones headed toward the rear. They found Cummings and Boyson, guarding the equipment that Wentworth and Jacobs had abandoned. The men were facing in opposite directions, watching for the enemy.

Tynan pointed at Boyson and said, "You stay."

"Sir," he said, "I think that I should be allowed to participate in this."

"You are," countered Tynan, a hard edge to his voice. "You are guarding the rear and the equipment. If we should fail, then you must destroy it all rather than letting it fall into the enemy's hands."

Boyson stared at Tynan, his face an angry mask, but he said nothing. He nodded his acceptance of the assignment.

Tynan then said to Cummings, "Let's catch up to the others."

"Aye aye, sir," said Cummings. He had swapped his M16 for one of the captured AK-47s. He had put on a chest pouch with three spare magazines. But he didn't carry the rifle in his hands. He slung it over his back diagonally so that it was held tightly against him. In his right hand he held his combat knife, the blade pointed up.

They moved off toward where Wentworth and Jacobs were keeping the enemy patrol in sight.

As Tynan and the others marched off to meet the enemy, Boyson was livid with rage. Tynan gave all the good assignments to his friends and left Boyson in the rear to guard the equipment. Given half a chance, he would prove that he was worthy. He'd stayed with them on the march in, he hadn't made noise, and he hadn't screwed up. But even that wasn't enough. Now Tynan and his men were off to meet the enemy threat head-on while he was stuck watching the equipment.

Boyson stood up near the trunk of a palm tree and watched as the SEALs disappeared into the jungle. When they were out of sight, he looked at the equipment and set about moving it from plain sight, concealing it with branches whittled from the bushes around him.

Finished with that, Boyson moved to the palm tree and leaned back against it. He searched the surrounding jungle, looking for signs of life. There were birds in the trees. Monkeys scampered around. Insects buzzed and the branches of the bushes and trees rattled with a light breeze.

But then, from the north and east came another sound. A quiet noise that could have been a voice. Boyson dropped to one knee and snapped the safety off his rifle. Then he remembered that Tynan had wanted to maintain silence.

He put his weapon down, leaning it against the trunk of the tree. He unsnapped his knife and pulled it out. Knife fighting wasn't something that the Army taught. They showed men how to use a bayonet attached to the end of a rifle. They were taught to use rifles, pistols, hand grenades, and machine guns. He even knew some unarmed techniques for fighting without weapons, but that was more of a joke than of any use. And he knew almost nothing about using a knife.

He tried to remember what he had learned in those few classes. Most of it was how to take out a guard from behind, but it was designed to break his neck and his back. Boyson was uncomfortable standing there with his knife in his hand. He wasn't sure he could use it. A rifle, fired into the trees where there wasn't much of a target, he could do. Easily. Didn't worry about it.

He could even aim at a man-shaped target a hundred yards away and try very earnestly to kill him. But now he was contemplating killing someone at close range. Killing a man with a knife was a very personal thing to do.

For a moment, he thought that his mind had been playing tricks on him. No one was coming. It had been a trick of the wind and the jungle.

And then he saw a movement in front of him. He turned his head slowly and stared. One man walked by and then a second. The first stopped, said something to the second, and then started moving again. They were headed almost directly at Boyson.

The easiest thing would be to pull his pistol and shoot them both. Two quick shots and the problem would have solved itself. But the shots would make too much noise.

Slowly Boyson slipped to one knee, using the bushes to screen himself from the enemy soldiers. He knew that they were soldiers and not innocent farmers because both carried old rifles, probably taken off the bodies of the French soldiers years earlier.

The leader turned slightly, moving off to the side. He avoided Boyson and, in fact, didn't see him. As he walked by, Boyson slipped to the right. The other man sensed something and turned, but Boyson froze, not moving. As the man shifted around, walking away, Boyson struck.

He grabbed the man from the rear, felt his hand slip, and then seized the shoulder of the uniform. He snapped his hand back, pulling the enemy soldier from his feet. As the VC fell backwards, Boyson plunged the knife into the man's chest.

The enemy started to scream and Boyson clapped a hand over the man's mouth. He bucked then, trying to toss Boyson to the side. One hand grabbed Boyson's trying to rip the knife from his chest. Boyson leaned over, using his weight to hold the knife in the struggling man. He twisted the blade and pulled it free then. Blood spurted as the blade came out, a crimson fountain that stained Boyson's clothes and splashed his face. The odor of fresh blood overwhelmed everything else in the jungle.

The downed soldier tried to throw Boyson off him with a single, final, mighty shove. Boyson lost his balance and fell to his side. The VC tried to sit up. There was a bubbling from his chest and blood poured from the wound. He groaned quietly and slipped to his side, pulling his legs up as he died.

The first enemy turned to find out what was happening. He called out quietly in Vietnamese. Boyson came up on his knees and tried to spot that man. He rocked back and wiped the blood from his face and his hands.

The VC approached slowly, searching for his

friend. His weapon was still slung because he didn't expect trouble. When he was close, Boyson stood up in front of him. One hand shot out, grabbed the front of the man's uniform as the other drove the knife into the soldier's belly, ripping upward. There was a stench of bowel that rose between the two men. The injured soldier stumbled to the rear, both hands clasped on the wound in his stomach.

He sat down, blood pouring between his fingers. Boyson moved in for the kill, but the wounded VC looked up at him. His face was almost blank and his skin suddenly waxy, as if he had been created only moments before. He grinned at Boyson and blood poured from his mouth. He slumped over, dead before he hit the ground.

Boyson stepped back then. He stared down at his handiwork. Two men dead of knife wounds. Not clean, efficient wounds, but deadly and silent, nonetheless. He crouched over the latest victim and pulled the rifle from his shoulder. He patted the pockets, searching for documents that would be of value to intelligence officers. The act was almost routine, unconscious. He had been told over and over that the dead could provide information that would be important. If there was a chance, the bodies should be searched.

But Boyson didn't want to stick his hands in the enemy's pockets. There was too much blood and the smell from the bodies was already beginning to make him sick. Instead, he rolled one up next to the tree and then pulled the other so that it was lying on the first. He wiped the blade of his knife on the uniform of the top man and then sheathed it.

He stood there for a moment, staring at the dead men, and realized that he felt nothing for them. They had walked up, paying no attention to the jungle around them and had died because of their inattention. Now they were dead at Boyson's hand, but he didn't brood about it. If they had been quicker, smarter, he'd be lying there dead instead.

Again he wiped a hand across his face and then moved away from the dead men. He stepped to the right where there was a palm tree and bent to pick up his rifle, but it wasn't there. He looked around and realized that he was looking in the wrong place. He moved again, to the next tree and still couldn't find his weapon.

For five minutes he searched the jungle, knowing it had to be close because he hadn't moved that far. Suddenly he understood the instruction that the old timers gave the FNGs. Never set your rifle down, because you'll lose it. The jungle was a confusing place filled with trees, bushes, flowers, and ferns that all looked the same. Setting your weapon down to piss was enough to lose it because it was so easy to get turned around in the jungle.

Then he found it, leaning against the palm. He grabbed it and crouched there, his back to the tree. Under his breath, he said, "Okay. Come on."

It took them almost no time to catch up with Wentworth and Jacobs. They could hear the enemy soldiers moving through the jungle ahead of them, though they weren't close enough to see them. Tynan used his binoculars, but the vegetation was too thick.

Wentworth came back and whispered to Tynan, "We've got twelve men moving slowly. Seems to be a paymaster or maybe an inspector general. Not your normal ragtag patrol."

"Where are they heading?"

Wentworth pointed. "They're moving off to the southwest now."

Tynan nodded and then put away the binoculars. "Let's get going."

Wentworth returned to where he'd left Jacobs. The big man was kneeling at the base of a tree, his rifle in one hand. When Tynan approached, he said, "I've got them about a hundred yards ahead of us."

"Go," said Tynan.

Jacobs began to work his way forward. The others strung out, creeping through the jungle, moving quietly. They stalked the other patrol, watching it through gaps in the vegetation and listening to it as it worked its way farther west.

Tynan got close enough to catch glimpses of the soldiers dressed in khaki uniforms. But unlike those worn in South Vietnam, these had badges of rank and insignia. Tynan recognized the shoulder boards of an NCO and saw the strange insignia of the cavalry, crossed sabers over a horseshoe.

Those men stopped for a moment and spread out into the jungle. There was a burst of quiet talking and several of the man lit cigarettes. As they settled in for a break, Jacobs retreated slightly to talk with Tynan.

"Looks like they're going somewhere else."

Tynan knew Jacobs meant that the route of march would no longer take them toward the small camp and tunnel system that Boyson was watching for them.

"I don't like leaving anyone around who could come back to haunt us later."

"You mean we're going to take them?"

Now Tynan shrugged. "We could lose the element of surprise if we get into a firefight here."

"We can't take them now with only knives. Too

many of them and some of them are liable to shoot anyway."

That suddenly gave Tynan an idea. "If you were at home and heard M16s firing, but no AKs or RPDs, what would your reaction be?"

"Figure some target practice was going on somewhere."

"And if you were in a sanctuary where you know the Americans can't operate, you'd tend to ignore AKs firing."

"Yes sir, I suppose."

Tynan grinned. "Then that's the answer. We use AKs to hose down the area and then get the hell out. If the enemy elsewhere hears nothing, fine, and we've eliminated a thorn in our sides."

"Aye aye, sir."

Tynan whirled and hurried to the rear. He found the others and whispered his instructions to them. They would fan out, forming an L-shaped force, move closer, and open fire on the enemy, using the AKs. Once that had been accomplished, they would retreat to the tunnel opening. With the plan explained, he asked for questions. There were none.

The men moved out. Jacobs had kept an eye on the enemy, who showed no signs of moving. The tiny unit spread out, working their way through the trees and bushes until they were all looking down at the enemy camp.

Tynan flipped off the safety of his AK and sighted on the officer who seemed to be the leader of the enemy. He waited until he was sure that he wouldn't miss and squeezed the trigger.

The shot took the man high in the chest, spinning him and then throwing him to the ground. Two of the enemy soldiers leaped to their feet, as if they couldn't believe what they had just seen.

As that happened, the other SEALs opened fire on full auto. The sounds of shooting ripped through the calm of the jungle. Birds scattered and monkeys fled screaming. The bullets smashed into the tiny band of enemy soldiers, tearing at their flesh and throwing them to the ground.

One or two of the Vietcong tried to get to their own weapons, but the ambush caught them all by surprise. The men danced under the impact of the bullets and were thrown to the ground. Blood spurted and stained their uniforms. Not one of them managed to get a shot off in retaliation.

As quickly as it started, it ended. The dead were sprawled on the jungle floor as the last of the echoes died away. It was suddenly as quiet as a tomb in the jungle. Even the insects had fallen silent.

Tynan moved forward slowly, out onto the field. He crouched over the closest body. It was badly damaged, the bullets having ripped through it. One hand was missing and the head was misshapen, as if slammed by a huge hammer.

Tynan picked up the weapon but then dropped it back on the ground. They already had more weapons than they could carry and another dozen or so would be a burden big enough to break their backs.

From the other end of the ambush, Jacobs moved over the field, checking the enemy. As Tynan stood, Jacobs shook his head. All the enemy soldiers were dead. They had been caught and killed before they had a chance to fight back.

"Let's get out of here," said Tynan.

"Weapons and intelligence," said Jacobs.

"No time for that. We've got to get back to Boyson

and see if we can get into the tunnels. Our time is running out now."

Jacobs turned and headed into the jungle. Without a word, the men fell in and began to work their way back the way they had come.

Tynan hesitated for a moment, staring at the ambush site. He didn't like leaving the bodies of the men scattered where they fell. Each man deserved a decent burial so that his body wasn't eaten by scavengers. An even better reason for burying the dead was so that the enemy wouldn't find them and know that Americans were in the area. But even that wasn't a good enough reason to hang back. In hours they would be on their way into South Vietnam and it wouldn't matter then if the enemy knew they were around.

He turned and hurried after the rest of his patrol. The enemy would have to take care of their own dead. Tynan had his own problems.

10

Sinclair sat in the tiny cage, watching his captors as they walked in front of them. None of them seemed interested in him either as a prisoner of war or as a representative of the American military. They were more interested in joking with one another.

He sat with his back against the hard earth of the wall. He couldn't stand up and he couldn't lie down. He was hunched over, staring out through the iron bars over the mouth of his cage. There was a bucket of water sitting on the floor five or six feet from his cage with a dipper in it. There was no way he could get to it for a drink and he was sure that was the purpose of its being there.

The officer who had spoken to him earlier finally returned. He crouched in front of the cage and peered into it. He grinned broadly and said, "Your discomfort is not necessary. If you'll answer my questions, then you may have some food and some water. Why make it difficult on yourself? No one will ever know what was said here."

Sinclair was not sure how he should react. If he was going to escape, he would need the water and food. If he was going to escape, he would have to get out of the cage. It was his duty to try to escape, but the Code of Conduct was also explicit in its instructions. He was to give nothing to the enemy.

So rather than answer, he closed his eyes and pretended that he couldn't hear the man outside the cage. He pretended that he was asleep.

The man stood up and a moment later a chair was brought for him. He sat down and tugged at the creases of his khaki trousers. He smiled and said nothing.

Sinclair watched that through slitted eyes. He didn't want the man to know that he was watching but his curiosity got the best of him. One thing bothered him greatly. Here was an enemy officer who was living in an underground tunnel and yet he was in a clean dress uniform that looked as if it had been pressed recently.

"You will not have to betray your fellows. I want only the most basic information, not specifics." He laughed. "Your own press provides us with the details."

Sinclair didn't respond to that. He was sure that it was true. He'd seen the details of their operations in the *Stars and Stripes* and was sure that those same stories appeared in newspapers in the World. But that made no difference. He was not going to say a word to the enemy.

"Sergeant Sinclair, you are only making this harder on yourself. There is no reason for your continued silence. If you do not cooperate, I'm afraid that there is nothing I can do for you."

"Sinclair, David . . ."

"Please, do not insult me with this anymore." He grinned. "But I have learned that you can still speak."

Sinclair decided that since he had already broken his self-imposed silence, he might as well make it worth his while. "I need water."

"Of course you do, Sergeant. But first I think that we must have some signs of cooperation on your part."

"Water," repeated Sinclair.

"Stalemate," said the officer. He rocked back in his chair and smiled. "But I can be magnanimous." He reached down and pulled the dipper from the water bucket. He moved to the door of the cage and added, "I will give you some water, but I expect something in return for it."

Sinclair leaned forward and took the dipper. He thought about the officer's words. He looked at the water in the dipper and thought that nothing had ever looked so good and inviting. There was plenty in the dipper, it would quench his thirst. But he didn't know what he could tell the officer. If he drank the water, he would owe the man something.

"Drink up," said the officer.

Still Sinclair hesitated.

Again the officer laughed. "Go ahead, Sergeant. Drink the water and we'll talk."

There didn't seem to be anything wrong with that. Sinclair put the dipper to his lips and tasted the water. It was warm but Sinclair didn't care. He drank it all and then handed the dipper back through the bars.

"Now, Sergeant, you can see that we are not bar-

barians as we are portrayed by your own Army. Please tell me your unit of assignment."

"I am forbidden to give that information," said Sinclair. "I am ordered to give only my name, rank, service number, and date of birth."

"Sergeant, we are not interested in making you betray your comrades. We understand that you feel kinship with them. But you are in my homeland killing my fellows. All we want is for you to show that you are willing to admit your mistakes and that you feel remorse for your actions."

Sinclair wanted to tell the man that he did feel remorse for his actions, but only because they had led to his capture. He felt he was right for fighting in South Vietnam, having seen some of the atrocities committed by the communists, but he knew better than to say so to the enemy officer. Silence was probably the best course.

The Vietcong officer sat there for a few minutes more, speaking to Sinclair, but when Sinclair refused to answer him, he gave up. He stood, looking down at Sinclair, and said, "Sergeant, you would be advised to cooperate with me because I am much more lenient than others who could be called in to talk to you. Some of them will not be as kind and will use torture to learn what they wish to know."

Sinclair didn't move.

"Well, you think about it, Sergeant. You decide whether you want to remain with us, or be moved to a camp where they are interested only in information."

The man picked up the water bucket and carried it away. At first Sinclair thought that it had been a bad move, but then realized it was better than leaving it in sight. Now he thought about it all the time. Before, he only thought about it some of the time.

Tynan and his SEALs worked their way back to where they had left Boyson and the equipment. Tynan moved out of the jungle, searching for Boyson, afraid that something had happened to the Army lieutenant.

Boyson appeared then and asked, "What happened? I heard shooting."

Tynan ignored the question. "How loud?"

"Not very," he said. "In the distance. You guys step into it?"

"We eliminated the enemy patrol. Couldn't afford to leave them running around loose behind us and didn't have the men to keep an eye on them. Anything happen here?"

Boyson turned and walked toward the trees where he'd left the bodies. He pointed them out to Tynan.

"What in the hell happened here?"

"They came strolling up, no idea of what was going on. I had to take them."

"You shoot them?" asked Tynan.

"I was afraid that would alert anyone hiding in the tunnels. Used my knife."

Tynan looked down at the dead men. Neither one looked to be older than twenty, though that didn't matter now. They'd played the game and lost.

"Well done," said Tynan.

"Thank you."

"No other activity around here?"

"No sir. It's been quiet. I don't think they can hear much once they're down there. We could get into a raging firefight and they wouldn't know it until someone stuck his head up to see what the weather was."

"You might be right." Tynan turned and headed off to where the rest of his men waited. When Boyson joined them, Tynan looked into their faces and asked, "Anyone have an idea on how to do this?"

Jones, who was eating some of the dried rations they had brought with them said, "We have to open the trapdoor and then someone has to drop down there."

"Great," said Jacobs. "You want to be the first?"

Jones grinned and said, "That sounds like something the officers should do."

Tynan rubbed a hand over his eyebrow. He squinted so that it looked as if his head ached. "I wouldn't think we'd want to waste high-priced and highly skilled officers in a job that the enlisted pukes could handle."

"The really good officers are leaders," said Jacobs. "They go first, showing the enlisted pukes that they're the bravest of the brave."

"Great," said Tynan. "That means I can forget about asking for volunteers."

"I would think so," said Jones.

Tynan turned and looked at the center of the area where the trapdoor was hidden. He stared at it, trying to figure out the best method of cracking it. There were tunnel rats who operated in South Vietnam, making their living by exploring the tunnels. Small men who went in with only a flashlight and a pistol. Suddenly Tynan understood just how brave those men were. There was something almost mind numbing about entering a hole in the ground with nothing but a pistol and flashlight.

"I say we have two or three men go in while the

rest stay up here to hold the trapdoor. When we're finished below, we retreat back to here."

"I'll stay up here," said Jones immediately.

"I'm afraid not," said Tynan. "You're thin enough that you're perfect for the tunnels."

"I'll go too," said Boyson.

"I don't know . . ."

"Come on, Tynan. You left me behind and I proved myself. Stopped those two men without using my rifle. Besides, I'm thin too. Thinner than you. I'd make a good tunnel rat. And it's my man down there."

"We don't know that," said Tynan.

"Then I'll take the benefit of the doubt. It's probably my man down there."

There didn't seem to be a rush of volunteers, so Tynan nodded. "From here I'm open to any and all suggestions that anyone might have."

No one spoke. They were all at a loss as to how to get into the tunnel system. One guard, sitting at the bottom of the entrance, was all that the enemy needed to alert them that the Americans were coming.

Tynan tried to envision what the inside of the tunnel complex would look like. All that came to him were memories from the movie *The Great Escape*, with the tiny tunnel dug by the English POWs in their attempt to get out. Tiny tunnels barely large enough to crawl through, with no place to turn around, and weak ceilings that collapsed regularly. It was not a place Tynan wanted to go, but there was no choice.

"I'll go first," said Tynan. "I'll take my pistol, a hand grenade, and a flashlight. Boyson, you're next, and Jones, you bring up the rear."

"Aye aye," said Jones. He didn't sound thrilled with the orders.

Tynan looked at his watch. He rubbed his lips with the back of his hand, took a deep breath, and said, "We'll stay down there no more than thirty minutes. After that, we'll get out. Jacobs, I want you to be prepared to take point and get us a good four or five clicks away. We'll want to head back toward South Vietnam."

"If we don't find anything in those thirty minutes?" asked Boyson.

"Then it's hopeless," said Tynan. "We've got to get out in thirty minutes."

"How we going to do this?" asked Jones. He was sweating heavily, but it wasn't from the heat or the humidity.

"Drop all our gear. Pistols and flashlights and maybe a grenade. Any shooting and we get out."

Tynan stood there for a moment and then said, "There must be something else, but I'm damned if I can think of it. Anyone have any thoughts at all?"

When no one said a word, Tynan shrugged. "Okay. Jacobs, deploy the men around the trapdoor. When you're set, we'll move in, low and slow."

Jacobs stood there for a moment and then said, "This isn't the greatest idea I've heard."

"Nothing we can do about it now," said Tynan. "Go."

Jacobs looked at Cummings and Wentworth and said, "Circle around to the west and take a position in the trees over there. Ten or fifteen meters apart, but close enough so you can support one another.

"Hernandez, take the north side. I'll take the south. Skipper, give us about twelve, fifteen minutes to get into position."

"Take a radio," said Tynan. "I'll take one, too.

Might not do any good, but it sure as hell won't hurt."

Jacobs nodded and pulled a URC-10 out of the equipment pile. He grabbed a second one and gave it to Tynan. "Thanks."

Jacobs, along with the others, took off then, moving through the jungle and into position. Tynan sat down, his back to a palm tree, and took a deep drink out of his canteen. He waited a moment and then took a second. Finished, he handed the canteen to Jones, who drank and passed it to Boyson.

When Boyson had finished, he said, "I'll go first."

"No," said Tynan. "The enlisted pukes were right about that. I should lead and by God I'm going to."

"Suit yourself."

Tynan glanced at his watch. The sweep second hand crawled around the face. Tynan didn't care. He wasn't anxious to start. He'd had a lot of different assignments since he'd become a SEAL but this was the worst one. He'd had no training to prepare for it. He would have to feel his way along and in combat the slightest mistake could kill quickly. There would be no second chances.

Finally the time was up. Tynan stood and stripped his equipment, dropping his harness and pistol belt to the ground. He took the Browning from his holster and made sure that a round was chambered. He found a spare magazine and put it in the pocket of his pants, figuring that if he needed it, he would be in too much trouble to get himself out. He stuffed the grenades into his pockets, hoping he wouldn't need them once he got down into the tunnel system. Last, he looked at his flashlight and pulled the red lens from it. In the tunnel he'd want all the light he could get.

"Ready?" he asked.

Jones shook his head. "No."

"Too bad."

Boyson took off his fatigue shirt. He held a .45 in one hand and a flashlight in the other. "I'm set."

"Let's take it very easy," said Tynan. "And when I say we get out, we get out."

Without waiting for an answer, Tynan got down to begin crawling forward. He moved carefully, lifting himself off the ground and then sliding just above it, holding himself up on his elbows, knees, and feet.

Boyson followed and then Jones. They worked their way out toward the center of the parklike area, Tynan in front, searching for signs of the trapdoor and keeping his eyes open, waiting for enemy soldiers to suddenly pop up. When he reached the center, he stopped, looked around, and spotted a slight depression to his right. He crawled to it and found the edge of the trapdoor. If they had been in South Vietnam, it wouldn't have been that simple, but in Cambodia, Charlie felt he was completely safe.

When both Boyson and Jones caught up, Tynan reached out. He worked his fingers under the edge of it. He turned and looked at each of the men and then flipped the door up out of the way, exposing the tunnel.

Tynan didn't know what to expect, but nothing happened. He eased his way closer and peered down inside. He could see the bottom of the pit and the three exits from them. He slipped back away from the edge.

"Three exits," he whispered.

"Each takes one," said Boyson.

"No," responded Tynan. "We've got to stay together. We'll explore one and then get out."

Boyson was going to protest, but Tynan silenced

him with a single, sharp look. Before he moved, Tynan said, "Let's keep it tight."

He crept to the edge, then looked down again. He shifted around so that he was sitting on the edge. He pushed himself off, dropping to the bottom of the pit. One by one, he looked down the tunnels that led from the pit. Dirt floors that looked as if they had been swept. Nothing to distinguish one from the other. Three tunnels, down which there could be death or an American prisoner. No time to explore them all and nothing to tell them apart.

He glanced up and saw Jones staring at him. There wasn't enough room to shrug. Instead, he faced each of the tunnels in turn and tried to figure out which way to go, but there was nothing unusual about any of them.

Then, just before he made the random choice, he noticed a cool breeze coming up at him. Fresh air from one of the tunnels. It could mean that the other two were traps. One that led deeper into the tunnel complex.

He turned and looked up at Jones, pointing into the tunnel. He then thumbed back the hammer of his pistol and leaned forward. He put his elbows on the edge of the tunnel and stared down. Now he could feel the breeze and smell the air. Not the odor of an open grave as he had expected. Charlie had done a good job of ventilating his tunnels.

He stretched and began crawling forward. He heard Boyson drop into the pit behind him and knew that the clock had started. Thirty minutes and they could start working their way out. Suddenly he hoped to survive for thirty minutes.

11

As soon as he had crawled all the way into the tunnel, he heard Boyson drop into the pit behind him. The shaft was so narrow that he couldn't turn to look. He couldn't even lift his head to see behind him. He'd have to take it on faith. Boyson and then Jones would be following him.

He pulled himself deeper into the tunnel. The sides looked as if they had been plastered with concrete, smoothed out carefully, and then swept free of dirt. It was cooler, cleaner, and fresher than he would have believed possible. The Vietcong had taken the ability to tunnel and turned it into a modern art form.

After only a few feet, he came to another huge opening. Another pit, ten feet across. He glanced down into what he had expected to be blackness and saw light bleeding into the tunnel complex. Not the flickering light of candles, or the bright, white light of lanterns, but the softer, yellower light of electricity. That was something else he hadn't expected.

Fastened to the wall of the pit, two or three feet away, was a ladder leading down. He could reach out, grab the rungs, and haul himself out of the tunnel. For a moment he hesitated, wondering if it was some kind of trap. The tunnels in South Vietnam were filled with false holes, booby traps, venomous snakes staked to the walls to bite anyone who entered.

But this was Cambodia and Charlie wasn't worried about the Americans. There was no reason to booby-trap anything. International law and American military regulations kept the Americans out of Cambodia.

Tynan wasn't sure he wanted to risk his life on logic. It wasn't logical that he would be down the tunnel in Cambodia, but there he was. Maybe the enemy booby-trapped the tunnels for the practice it would give them. Or maybe they did it in case American policy changed suddenly and radically.

He felt Boyson come up behind him. He was aware of all of them in the tunnel now. Maybe it was the sound of the breathing that seemed to swell as the walls focused the noise.

Tynan reached out, grasped the ladder, and pulled himself from the tunnel. Slowly, he put his weight on it. First it was just one hand and then a foot, and finally he was standing on the ladder, his pistol in his right hand, his flashlight clipped to his waistband.

As he started down, he looked Boyson right in the face. The Army lieutenant didn't look comfortable. The little light filtering up the shaft from below showed that Boyson was sweating heavily although it was cool in the tunnels. His skin was very white, standing out in stark contrast to his dark hair and the darker environment in the tunnel.

Without a word, Tynan started down. When he was close to the bottom, he stopped and bent, hanging on to one of the higher rungs, trying to see into the tunnel there. Convinced that there was no one waiting in ambush, he dropped from the ladder.

The sight that greeted him stunned him. He had expected another tiny shaft, barely large enough for him to crawl through, but that wasn't the case. Although the opening was only three feet in diameter, it opened up into a larger tunnel, ten or twelve feet across.

"Christ," he mumbled. He then looked up and saw that Boyson was coming down the ladder.

Tynan crawled through the opening and then moved to the right and stood up. He studied the chamber, which had a wooden floor and sleeping pallets carved into the wall. The air was fresh and cool and if they had brought in radios, it would have been better than the bunkers and tents used by Americans in South Vietnam.

Boyson stuck his head in and said, "What the fuck?"

"Quiet."

Tynan moved across the floor, staying close to the tunnel entrance. His eyes were on the entrance at the far end. As he moved, he noticed that there was very little left behind. There were no weapons, no personal gear. The remains of a magazine printed in the United States and a single, empty C-ration can. Nothing that would be of use to him or anyone else.

He reached the far end and crouched. Carefully, he looked out and found another darkened shaft. Part of it went lower, but it looked as if the bottom was filled with water. Going up was a ladder that led to another tunnel. There was more light coming from there.

Tynan turned and saw that Jones had joined them. He wasn't sure he liked having everyone in the same tunnel at once, but there didn't seem to be a good reason to keep them out. He pointed at Boyson and waved him forward, signaling him to stop at the entrance. He then pointed at Jones and motioned him to stay put for a moment.

When Boyson was in place, Tynan entered the shaft. He glanced down at the water and then began climbing up to the next level. He stopped short, crouched on the ladder, and listened. There was a quiet hum, coming from the generator hidden somewhere else. He could also hear voices, but they seemed to be far away from him.

Finally, he stood up so that his eyes were just above the level of the floor. Again he was looking into a large, open area with a slat floor and the smooth bore walls of a tunnel. A shadow moved on the wall, telling him that there was someone in the tunnel.

He ducked down and tried to figure out what to do. If he shot the man, everyone in the tunnel complex would hear the shot. There was no way to get to him without exposing himself. He needed a silenced pistol and the military wouldn't let him have one, except under special circumstances. Silencers were against regulations.

There was a noise above him and Tynan looked up just as the man there looked down. There was a startled look on the man's face. Tynan's empty hand shot up, grabbed the shirt of the enemy soldier, and yanked him free from the tunnel. Tynan flattened himself against the wall of the shaft as the body hurtled by. The man began a scream that was cut off abruptly as he hit the surface of the water.

Tynan didn't give the man a chance to react. He dropped feet first from the ladder, landing on the back of the enemy. He held him down under the water as he struggled to get clear. One hand clawed at the smooth wall. He bucked, kicked, and splashed, but Tynan wouldn't let him up. Slowly the struggles tapered and then stopped. There was a bubbling in the water as the last of the air escaped the man's lungs.

Tynan reached down into the dark water, and felt for a pulse at the man's neck, but there was none. He then felt the knife on the VC's belt and took it.

Boyson stuck his head out and Tynan held a thumb up. He then climbed back on the ladder. Again he peeked into the new chamber, but this time saw no shadows. There was no sound from it either. He was sure that if anyone had been in it, he would have heard the splash and rushed to investigate.

Confident that the tunnel was empty, Tynan climbed into it and looked into the face of an enemy soldier. The man was standing to one side of the tunnel. Dressed in black pajamas, he held an AK in his hands.

Tynan leaped at him, but the man danced away. He swung his rifle around and pulled the trigger. The bullet ripped through the air next to Tynan's head. He heard it whistle near him. Without thinking, he pointed his pistol and fired. The round hit the man in the sternum with a wet slap and a cracking of bone. The man dropped immediately, looking as if his bones had suddenly melted.

Tynan was up and moving then. He ran across the floor and looked into the next connecting tunnel. No one had appeared there yet, but Tynan was sure they would.

"Hey, get me out of here!"

Tynan turned and saw the cage then. Recessed in the shadows the way it was, it was easy to miss.

"Who the hell are you?" asked Tynan.

"Could ask you the same thing. My name's Sinclair. Now get me the hell out of here."

Tynan looked at the brass padlock that held the iron door in place. "He have a key?"

"What difference does that make. Shoot it off."

The logic was inescapable. Two shots had already been fired. A third wouldn't make that much difference. He moved to one side and aimed at the hasp. He pulled the trigger and the bullet whined off. The lock was hanging open.

Sinclair shoved the cage door open and scrambled across the floor to the AK the enemy had dropped. He worked the bolt, ejecting a single, live round. "Let's get out."

Tynan suddenly realized that the whole reason for being in the tunnels was to find the captive American and they had now retrieved him.

"There any more prisoners?"

"No. Not that I know of."

"Head back that way. You'll see another American."

"Got it."

Tynan moved to the opposite end and glanced up. Again he saw a shadow. He ducked back and then heard a voice calling in Vietnamese. He was sure that it was an NCO trying to learn what all the shooting was about.

As Sinclair reached the other side, he heard an American voice say, "What in the hell?"

"Hi, Lieutenant."

Tynan wanted to tell them to shut the fuck up, but that would make more unnecessary noise. If they were smart, they would be getting the hell out.

The shadow fell across the tunnel entrance again and Tynan aimed up at the opening. He waited patiently, trying not to blink. When a shape moved in front of the entrance, he pulled the trigger. There was a muffled shriek and a rifle fell into the open.

Just at that moment, the lights all went out. As they did, Tynan whirled and began to crawl along the floor as quickly as he could. His hand hit the foot of the man he had killed. He crawled over the body and reached the entrance.

Behind him, shooting erupted. An AK on full auto. Glancing over his shoulder, he could see the muzzle flashes looking like the strobe of a camera.

As he reached the ladder, there was shouting in Vietnamese. Tynan climbed out and then stopped. One man with a pistol could hold that position for hours. The enemy couldn't attack by force, and grenade would be ineffective. The Vietcong had outsmarted themselves on that point. If the grenade fell short, Tynan could duck, letting the shrapnel whistle overhead and if it was long, it would drop into the water below him.

"Skipper, you coming?"

"Get out," said Tynan.

"I'll wait with you," said Jones.

"No, get on out. That's an order."

"Aye aye."

Tynan turned his attention back to the darkened chamber. He could see nothing in it, it could be filled with enemy soldiers. Suddenly he realized the value of the grenade that he carried: he could use it to slow the pursuit and give himself a chance to get out.

He ducked, pulled his grenade, and yanked the pin free. He dropped the pin into the water below him.

Leaning forward, he stood up and, balancing himself on the ladder, he used his left hand, now holding his pistol, to locate the entrance to the tunnel. He leaned into it and tossed the grenade underhand toward the center of the chamber. Then he ducked down again.

He heard the grenade hit the wooden floor and a moment later there was a single loud detonation that echoed through the tunnel complex. There were screams and an angry shout.

Tynan turned, scrambled down, and felt his way into the other tunnel. As he reached it, firing broke out behind him—AKs on full auto, echoing in the darkness. He leaped into the tunnel and sprawled flat, listening. None of the bullets were coming close to him. They were hitting the walls of the shaft where he had been hiding.

"Skipper?"

"I'm fine. Go."

A light flashed in front of him. Tynan used that to orient himself and crawled across the floor. He reached the other end and saw that Boyson was on the ladder near the tunnel entrance. Sinclair was right behind him and Jones was using his flashlight.

"Move it!" yelled Tynan.

From the other direction, there was more shooting and shouting. No one there seemed to have any idea what was going on. They were shooting at shadows, imaginary shapes, and absolutely nothing at all.

Tynan climbed from the tunnel then and dropped to the bottom of the pit. "Let's go," he shouted up at them.

Jones pushed at Sinclair, who was trying to get into the tunnel. "Hurry," he said.

As Sinclair disappeared into the tunnel, Jones snapped off his light and began to scramble up the ladder. Tynan hesitated and then joined him, hurrying up.

The shooting from the other tunnel began to taper. There was more shouting and then an explosion. Not the loud crash of the American-made grenade, but a quieter, more subdued sound. A Chicom weapon that didn't have the punch or the shrapnel of its American counterpart. Tynan knew of men who had been standing next to Chicom grenades when they detonated, and who had only been slightly injured.

Jones left the ladder, crawling into the tunnel. Tynan was up there then, waiting for the man to clear the entrance. When he was out of the way, Tynan crawled in after him. The shooting began again. Looking back, he could see lights flashing in the tunnel and in the shaft. Some of them were the muzzle flashes of the firing AKs but there was also steady light from lanterns. The enemy was trying to get them before they got outside.

"Hurry it up," said Tynan. "They're coming."

The first of the shots rumbled up through the underground complex and burst into the night air. They were such quiet, muffled pops, no louder than the smallest of firecrackers, that Jacobs wasn't sure they were shots.

The radio crackled and Wentworth said, "I have movement over here."

Jacobs squeezed the mike button twice, acknowledging the call. Then came a second from Hernandez. More movement.

Jacobs lifted the radio to his lips and said, "Take them out if you have to. Quietly."

As he lowered the radio, there was a rustling in the jungle behind him. Jacobs put the radio into its case and then drew his combat knife. He slipped to the right and crouched among the branches of a large bush. They didn't conceal him completely, but they broke up the outline of his body, making it harder for the enemy to spot him.

A single man carrying an AK-47 moved through the jungle near him. Jacobs recognized the outline of the weapon but even without that, Jacobs knew the man was the enemy. He was too small to be an American and Jacobs knew where everyone else was.

The Vietcong stopped and crouched. His head turned slowly, almost as if he were a radar antenna searching for an electronic target. He stood up, moved to the right, and stopped again, searching the jungle for the Americans.

He went through the routine again and then moved closer to Jacobs. Now the big man could smell the smaller man. There had been talk that the American's use of after-shave and insect repellent made it possible for the enemy to smell them out, but this VC fell into the same trap. Jacobs could smell the insect repellent the man had spread on himself. That meant he wasn't at home in the jungle.

Again he moved so that he was within reach of Jacobs, who decided the time was right. As the soldier turned his head away from him, Jacobs struck. He leaped the few feet separating the two, grabbed the VC from behind, and lifted him from his feet. With one hand under the enemy's chin and the other on the back of his head, Jacobs jerked the head to the right and then to the left. He felt the snap of the neck and heard the breaking of bones. The enemy died with a sigh and the stench of bowel. Jacobs dropped the body to the ground and moved away quickly.

Suddenly he was aware of movement in the jungle

all around him. Not one man, but more. Five, or six, or maybe a whole squad. They seemed to have come from nowhere and were searching the jungle.

The radio crackled again but before a word was spoken, he shut it off. The last thing he needed was for the radio to give away his place of hiding.

From underground came the sound of more shots. A grenade detonated with a roar that filtered through the earth. Jacobs glanced at the trapdoor hidden in the center of the clearing, but there was no indication that the advance party was returning.

He turned and saw four men moving toward him. He shook his head because there was no way for him to silently eliminate them. He had to take them out because they would be in a position to grab the search party as it came up out of the ground. But rather than give away his position, he pulled a grenade, yanked the pin free, and then studied the terrain.

There was nothing between him and the enemy soldiers except some bushes and ferns. He cocked his arm, measuring the distance to the Vietcong, and then threw the grenade. Not a hard throw like an outfielder trying to nail the lead runner; more like the shortstop who needs to flip the ball to second.

As he released it, he dropped to the ground, covering his eyes with his arm. He didn't want to ruin his night vision with the flash from the grenade. He heard it hit the ground and heard a shout just before the explosion. As the grenade went off, firing erupted. There were screams of pain and cries of anguish. The muzzle flashes marked the hiding places of the surviving Vietcong.

Jacobs rolled to the left and plucked another grenade free. He threw it, hiding his face again. As it exploded, he leaped and ran farther to the left, diving for cover as the firing began again.

He rolled to the right, his back to the tree, and yanked his radio free of its pouch. He turned it on and said, "Enemy assault."

"Roger" came a single reply.

Then, suddenly, the jungle erupted with M16s and AK-47s. In the flashing, strobing light, he could see men moving with the jerky, unreal motion of an old movie. Three men were running across the ground, heading for the trapdoor entrance to the tunnel complex. Jacobs whirled, swinging his rifle from his side, his thumb flipping off the safety.

But before he could fire, someone else opened up. No more than half a dozen yards from the enemy soldiers, the muzzle flashes reached out. Long, yellow-orange tongues of flame that touched the stomachs and chests of the VC. The man went down, tumbling. There were more screams. And then the firing stopped for an instant.

Jacobs heard the bolt of an RPD slide home. He whirled and, with his AK on full auto, opened fire. The pulsing of the firing showed him the enemy soldiers, outlining them in relief. He saw them hit and tumble. They sprawled on the jungle floor and didn't move.

As soon as the enemy was down, he turned and leaped toward the tree. He touched the trunk and slipped to the ground, then crawled to the other side and stood up.

Firing broke out to the right. M16 against AK-47. In the darkness, with the Americans armed like the enemy and the VC having stolen M16s, he couldn't just fire until he identified the targets. That portion of the jungle looked like a lightning storm gone mad.

Flashing lights. Burning tracers, some red and some green. They crisscrossed. A grenade detonated, throwing a momentary fountain of glowing sparks and orange fire into the air.

Jacobs looked out into the jungle where the trap-door was hidden and saw light flash from it. A small, dim light, like that of the hand-held flashlights carried by Tynan and Jones.

"Stay down," he shouted. "Stay down."

He turned again and saw men rushing toward him —three or four dark shapes coming out of the jungle. It couldn't be other SEALs. They wouldn't be that stupid. He aimed his AK, waist high, and opened fire on single shot, pulling the trigger as fast as he could. The men stumbled and fell, rolling and screaming. He kept shooting into them until they were quiet. Then, not wanting to get killed, he ran to the right. As he did, the jungle erupted again, sparkling with the muzzle flashes of a dozen weapons firing into the empty air where he had been.

More of the enemy was showing up and each of them was firing. Grenades were going off around him. Dull, quiet pops, that were Chicom. There was the single roar of an American-made grenade and then the firing intensified. More weapons on full auto and the lumbering chug of a fifty-caliber machine gun.

Under his breath, Jacobs said, "Now where in the hell did they get that?"

And then the world seemed to catch fire and the only thing he could do was dive for cover and pray that he survived the night.

12

As Tynan grabbed the ladder and began to climb, he heard firing erupt behind him and then felt the ground around him vibrate. The explosion from the surface filtered down to him and he yelled up, "What in the hell is happening?"

Boyson called back, "Firefight."

Tynan wanted to shout, but didn't. He climbed up the ladder into the last tunnel. He crawled partially into it and then called, "Anyone have a grenade left?"

"Coming at you, Skipper," said Jones.

Tynan heard it rolling along the ground, but couldn't see a thing in the darkness. He put his hands out, spreading them wide, and the grenade rolled into it.

"Thanks."

He wished he could turn around but that was impossible. The best thing was to lie with his face in the opening and wait for the enemy to show himself.

When he knew they were there, drop the grenade on them.

Firing erupted above him. Grenades detonated. M16s and AKs were shooting. The battle above them became hotter as more weapons joined in.

Tynan couldn't stand it. He backed out of the tunnel to the ladder, then swung his feet up and in. He crawled backward so that he was facing down into the shaft. He watched and listened. There was more shouting below him, the voices coming closer. The timing would be critical.

Then, as if to announce that they were near, an AK opened fire. The glowing green tracers flashed out of the chamber and struck the wall of the shaft. They bounced and fell burning to the bottom of the pit. In the glow of the burning green, Tynan saw one man look up.

Without waiting, Tynan pulled the pin of the grenade and ducked. He hesitated. An AK opened up, the bullets striking around the entrance where he hid. He could hear them hitting the smooth walls, he could hear the dirt falling, and he could smell it, along with the burnt gunpowder.

The firing stopped and a voice called something out in Vietnamese. Still Tynan hesitated. And then he decided it was time. He reached out and let go of the grenade. It fell, striking the bottom of the pit. A moment later it went off with a deafening roar as the sound was focused and channeled by the walls of the tunnel and the shaft. Dust filled the chamber and Tynan coughed.

"Skipper," yelled Jones. "Skipper."

Tynan shook his head. His ears were ringing with the sound. He could barely hear the shouts behind him. They filtered down like the static-filled voices of friends on poor long-distance phone calls.

"Skipper?"

"I'm fine. Let's go."

Tynan began backing up then. He pushed himself away from the entrance. From below, he could hear nothing. The enemy had stopped shouting and stopped shooting.

He moved until he ran into another person. He tried to look over his shoulder and shouted, "What the hell?"

"We've got a firefight going on out there."

"We've got to get out," he said.

Jones passed on the message and Tynan heard a muffled reply. Then Jones repeated it: "Too much shooting."

"Get out as soon as you can," he said. Then, without waiting to hear what the others said, he began crawling back to the shaft. He could hold it for a long time. That was the least of their problems. Unless the enemy had a way to flank them. Maybe use one of the other tunnels.

Tynan waited and listened, but the shooting above him was filling the tunnels with noise. Grenades were shaking them, filling them with dust that swirled around, clogging the mouth and nose, and showed no sign of settling.

Finally Tynan reached out with his pistol and tried to aim straight down. He fired twice and jerked his hand back. He was rewarded with a scream and the sound of a body dropping. As he scrambled to the rear, firing from below erupted. Bullets smashed into the walls, shredding them.

"We'd better get out of here soon," said Tynan.

No one replied.

* * *

Cummings crouched among the lacy branches of the ferns and watched the flashing and flickering of the weapons as the enemy fired at the shadows. He moved forward to where he could see the open trapdoor and waited. There was a flash of light from it but no one appeared there.

He saw two men running across the open ground, heads down, looking like men running into a strong wind. One of them stopped, and as he did, Cummings opened fire. The first rounds struck the running man, dropping him to the ground. His partner turned toward Cummings, but Cummings kept shooting. The second fell to his side, tried to get up, and then died.

To the left was more firing and Cummings saw a shape there. He rolled over, so that he was next to the trunk of a tall tree, but didn't shoot.

"Bruce, where the fuck are you?"

"Here," said Cummings.

Wentworth appeared and crouched near him. "We've got to clear this area so the guys in the tunnels can get out."

"So what did you have in mind?"

"We need to swing to the north and cut down the opposition."

As he spoke, grenades started detonating. A machine gun opened fire, hammering away. A moment later it fell silent and the sound was replaced with the slow, steady pounding of a large-caliber weapon.

"Shit, that's a fifty."

"We've got to take it."

"Right," said Cummings, but he knew they would. It was the only way that the men in the tunnels could get out.

He surveyed the jungle until he spotted the muzzle flash from the fifty. The flame from the barrel was nearly ten feet long and was lighting up the ground like a Fourth of July display.

"Let's go," said Wentworth. Without waiting, he was on his feet moving.

Cummings followed. He bent low, watching the jungle around him. As Wentworth ran by a bush, a Vietcong hidden inside it opened fire. Wentworth seemed to leap forward, as if hit in the back by a two-by-four. He was lifted off his feet and then sprawled like a rag doll. Cummings slipped to a halt and hosed down the bush. The enemy soldier screamed once and fell into the open.

The fifty had stopped firing momentarily, but as Cummings hit the ground, it opened up again, the rounds flashing over his head. He hugged the jungle floor, the odor of rotting vegetation in his mouth and nose as he tried to dig a foxhole with his face. He rolled to the right, trying to get out of the line of fire.

Just as he did, someone yelled, "Grenade!" Over the sound of the fifty firing, he heard the bomb snap through the jungle. An instant later, it exploded and the fifty ceased firing. The shrapnel ripped through the jungle, shredding the trees and bushes.

Cummings was up and running then. He leaped over a bush and found himself facing the fifty, but the crew was scattered around it. One man was slumped over the butterfly trigger and two others were sprawled behind the gunner.

"Fifty's down," yelled Cummings.

"Yeah!" shouted Jacobs.

Cummings dropped to the ground and turned back toward the trapdoor. He saw another man creeping toward it and fired once, twice, three times. The man stopped moving, but Cummings didn't know if he had been hit or if he had just stopped.

Then another man came swarming out of the vegetation, his weapons held high. He was screaming at the top of his voice, the bayonet on his rifle pointed at Cummings. The SEAL swung his own rifle around to deflect the bayonet. As he did, he fell to the rear, rolling on his shoulder. He kicked out and felt his foot connect with the enemy. The man fell forward. Cummings scrambled up, put the barrel of his weapon to the back of the VC's head, and pulled the trigger.

As that soldier died, the firing around them began to taper off to sporadic shots and a few tracers. One lanced over the trapdoor, struck something and bounced upward, tumbling out of sight.

And then it was silent. Cummings got to his feet and looked down at the body of the dead man. In the dim light of the jungle, he could see the ragged black stain on the rear of the man's uniform. He turned and saw the bodies of the others, around the machine gun.

He moved forward to the edge of the vegetation where he could see out to the trapdoor. For a moment, nothing happened. Then one man lifted himself clear, stood up straight, and dived for cover.

An instant later, an AK opened fire, but the bullets were wide of the mark and someone else silenced the enemy before either Cummings or the man on the ground could react.

Tynan fired down the tunnel twice more, but didn't hit anyone. There was some return fire, but not much. With all the shooting going on above him, he knew that the VC knew they only had to prevent Tynan and his boys from using the tunnels to escape. There were only two ways out, one blocked by the

men in the tunnels below him and the other up
through the trapdoor.

"Skipper," said Jones, "firing's tapering."

"Then let's get out now."

He started pushing himself backward. He reached
Jones and stopped. He tried to look over his shoulder,
but it did no good. The tunnel wasn't wide enough to
allow him to do that.

He stretched out, his hands in front of him, the
pistol pointed down the tunnel. He stared down it,
waiting for an enemy soldier to appear there.

A moment later Jones called, "Let's go, Skipper."

Tynan backed up, bumped into Jones, and then
stopped. A moment later, Jones moved out into the
main shaft. Tynan slipped farther back, but kept his
eyes on the opposite entrance. Jones climbed out and
Tynan moved back. He was in the shaft and stood up.
He could see the others lying on the ground near him.

"Go!" he shouted.

As two of them leaped up, there was a burst of
machine-gun fire. Both dropped down and Tynan
ducked. Firing came from the jungle. M16s and AKs
again. A few bullets flashed over them.

"Go!" yelled Tynan. "Go!"

Boyson and Sinclair took off running. Jones turned
and held out a hand. Tynan grabbed it, Jones pulled
him from the pit. Jones then whirled and the two of
them followed Boyson and Sinclair.

As they reached the vegetation, they dropped to
the ground and watched the trapdoor. The firing was
rippling around them. Tynan spotted the muzzle
flashes. He pulled out his radio and said, "Let's pull
it in. Acknowledge."

He was rewarded with the double clicks from the

others. Tynan then turned and said, "Let's get a perimeter established."

Boyson and Sinclair moved deeper into the vegetation and took up positions. Tynan tried to get a feel for the number of enemy soldiers around them.

"Coming up from the tunnels," said Jones.

Tynan glanced and saw an enemy soldier poke his head out. He aimed his pistol at the man but didn't fire. He let that man get clear of the hole and, as the next one tried to climb out, he fired. The second enemy dropped back, out of sight.

As that happened, Jones fired three times. The enemy soldier dived for cover and tried to get back into the tunnel. Jones slipped to one knee and aimed carefully. He fired again and the enemy soldier stopped moving.

"Coming in," said a voice.

"Come ahead," said Tynan.

Jacobs crouched down and said, "Glad to see you, sir. How'd things go?"

"Fine. What's the status here?"

Jacobs rubbed the back of his hand on his lips and said, "We've got a bunch of VC running loose. Took out a fifty. I think we've beaten them back for now."

Tynan nodded and said, "Let's get out of here. To the east. We take any casualties?"

"I don't know. We're still scattered."

Boyson returned and said, "We've got movement behind us. Squad, maybe two."

"Okay," said Tynan. "Let's move off to the left. It clear that way, Jacobs?"

"Was when I came in."

"Then go. Boyson, you and Sinclair hold your position for sixty seconds and then withdraw. Quietly. Let's do it."

Jacobs vanished into the vegetation again. Jones followed and Tynan waited until he saw that Boyson and Sinclair were falling back. He then headed off after Jones and Jacobs. He caught up with them at the base of a huge teak tree.

As he arrived another voice said, "Coming in."

"Come ahead."

Cummings and Hernandez appeared then. Tynan looked at them. "Anyone know where Wentworth is?"

"Dead."

"You sure?"

"Positive."

"Can we get to the body?"

"No sir. Too many of the enemy around it. I took the precaution of smashing his teeth. Left a grenade under him."

"Okay," said Tynan. "Our first order of business is to get clear. Straight east, out of here."

Firing broke out again and Tynan ducked. Hernandez called, "Coming up behind us."

"Jacobs, take point."

"What about the equipment we left?"

"Fuck it. Let's get out of here. Now." Jacobs got up and moved into the jungle.

"Cummings, take up the rear. Jones, hang back with him. Boyson, you and Sinclair get going."

They took off and then Tynan moved out. Firing rippled through the area, but it was poorly directed. Tynan hurried off and then stopped. The rear guard started moving and Tynan hurried to catch the first group.

They got clear of the area. The firing faded in the background. Jacobs picked up the pace. He wasn't worried about leaving signs. He was only interested in getting the hell out.

Tynan caught up to him when he stopped near the bed of a stream that had dried up. Jacobs was kneeling on the ground, his compass out.

"East," said Tynan. "That's all you've got to know."

"Aye aye," he said.

He took off then, running as fast as he could. The patrol strung out behind him. They ran across the dry stream bed, up the bank, and out onto a game trail. They ran along it, dodging the trees and the bushes and the ferns. They ran as fast as they could in the dim light of the jungle. They rushed along, ignoring the heat and the humidity, no longer worried about making noise. Now it was only important to get back to South Vietnam.

They ran up a slight hill, over the top, and then down it. They ran across a flat plain and across a clearing where the grass was knee-deep and the starlight and moonlight from overhead made it nearly as bright as day. They entered the jungle, dodged right and then left, keeping the pace fast. They kept running until they could no longer hear the firing from the area of the trapdoor and until they were sure that the enemy wasn't racing after them.

Jacobs came to a stream that hadn't dried, and stopped there. Tynan caught up to him and dropped to the ground near him. The sweat popped out along his forehead and under his arms. It dripped, soaking his uniform. He was suddenly hot and thirsty. He wanted to take a drink, but his canteen, along with his backpack and other equipment, was still back at the trapdoor.

Jacobs, without saying a thing, handed his over and said, "Just don't drink it all."

Tynan took the canteen gratefully, tipped it to his lips, and filled his mouth with the warm, chemical-tasting water. He swallowed it and felt it all the way down until it spread in his stomach. He handed it back then.

"We're a click, maybe two, from the trapdoor."

"Puts us what? Ten from the border?"

"Something like that."

He looked around. The others were there: Jones and Cummings had taken up firing positions facing the rear in case they were jumped. Hernandez was watching one flank, Boyson the other.

Tynan moved back to Cummings and leaned close. "Wentworth was dead."

"Yes sir. I'm positive. I smashed his teeth with the butt of my pistol, flipped him over and put a grenade under his head. Enemy moves him and the grenade goes off. Should destroy all the evidence."

"Good," said Tynan. As he moved back to the front of the patrol, he realized what he had just said. To himself, he said that he wasn't glad that Wentworth was dead, but that his body would be of no use to the enemy.

As he crouched near Jacobs, he said, "Give it another ten minutes and then let's get going."

"With luck, by dawn, we'll be back inside South Vietnam."

Tynan nodded. "Let's slow it down a little bit. I don't want us running into an ambush now."

"Charlie wouldn't be setting ambushes in Cambodia. No one in Cambodia to ambush."

"I don't want to trust my life to that assumption.

We'll take it easy. Besides, Charlie knows that we're inside Cambodia now."

"No way he could get in front of us."

Tynan shook his head. "Charlie has radios and he has to know the direction we'd take to escape."

"So we'll be careful," said Jacobs.

Tynan stood up and looked to the east, but could see nothing other than more trees and jungle. Through a gap he could see part of the dark sky, the stars staring down at him.

"Tomorrow by this time we'll be back at Nha Be sucking down beer, but right now, we've got to be careful."

"Aye aye, sir."

Jones approached them then. He leaned close to Tynan. "Sir, I can't be sure, but I think we've got someone on our tail."

"Coming this way?"

"Yes sir."

"Jacobs, let's get going. Jones, you hang back, and if the enemy is coming toward us or seems to be following us, give us three clicks on the radio and then close it up."

"Aye aye, sir."

"Okay, let's get this show on the road." He was silent for a moment and then added, "And for God's sake, let's be careful. I don't want to lose anyone else."

13

Now they moved with more caution. Closer to the border, they knew that the Vietcong and the North Vietnamese would be alert for American intrusions. There had been skirmishes on the border, and Americans had crossed, moving as deeply as one click into Cambodia in pursuit of the enemy. Besides, the border was not marked, so either side might think they were on one side and be on the other.

The patrol collapsed toward the center so that everyone could support everyone else. The pace slowed and they could easily hear the firing of artillery in South Vietnam. There were distant booms that sounded like thunder in a storm several miles away.

Jacobs finally stopped again, taking a short break. When Tynan moved up to him, Jacobs whispered, "If we're not in South Vietnam yet, we're damned close."

Before Tynan could respond, Jones caught up and

said, "We've got someone definitely following us."

"You get any idea of who or how many?"

"No sir. They're very good, whoever they are. They're staying a hundred, two hundred meters behind us. Just pick up an occasional noise from them."

"I don't like this," Tynan whispered. "The only reason to follow us is so that someone could set up an ambush in front of us. We're going to have to take them out."

"What are you planning, Skipper?"

"Jacobs, you continue on point. Lead the men straight east another click or so and then stop to wait. Jones, Cummings and I will stay back and ambush the VC. Once we've caught up, we'll veer south or north and should be able to avoid anything the enemy has arranged."

Cummings came up and said, "Those guys behind us are getting closer."

"Jacobs, you'd better go. Jones, you have a radio?"

"Yes sir."

"If we really step on it, we'll call. I'll break squelch three times as we come in."

"Got it."

"Then go," said Tynan.

As Jacobs moved out, with Boyson and Sinclair behind him and Hernandez bringing up the rear, Tynan, Jones, and Cummings spread out. Cummings and Jones took the long axis of the L-shaped ambush, with Tynan on his own as the base.

Then they stopped moving. Tynan, crouched on one knee, leaned against the smooth trunk of a teak tree. He braced his shoulder against it, holding his rifle in both hands. His thumb nervously touched the safety on the side of his rifle. He kept his eyes on the trail, trying to memorize each of the bushes, ferns, trees, and shadows. A light breeze stirred the leaves of the trees so that there was a quiet rustling and the shadows shifted around.

Tynan studied that and the jungle. He felt the sweat drip as the heat radiated from his body. Running through the jungle—and then suddenly stopping—made him hot and miserable. It made it seem hotter than it was. He wanted to wipe away the sweat and fan his face, but didn't want to move. The slightest movement could draw attention to himself and that was the last thing he wanted.

It wasn't long before the enemy soldiers who were following neared. Tynan heard them first. A quiet rustling coming toward them. Not much of a sound. One that would have been lost in the breeze if he hadn't been listening for it.

Then he saw the first of the enemy soldiers moving toward him. A hunched shape, distinctive because of the pith helmet he wore. There was a shadow that was obviously his AK, the banana clip extending down and curving toward the front.

The man came closer, stepping carefully, watching where he was going. A second appeared behind him and then a third. That man carried a radio, but he was not using it and there was no sound from it.

Slowly, Tynan shifted his rifle around so that the barrel was pointing at the enemy soldiers, the safety off. He glanced away once, almost as if he were afraid he would communicate the ambush to them through ESP. He didn't want the enemy to get any kind of warning.

They came on, a fourth and fifth man looming out of the darkness of the jungle. They were staggered, not following one behind the other, and they were moving slowly. Their heads were swiveling right and left as they searched the vegetation for some sign that the Americans were close.

The point man was in the killing zone of the tiny ambush, and then, almost immediately, out of it. Tynan saw that a sixth man had appeared, but that seemed to be the end of the short column. He shifted again, aimed at the back of the point man, and slowly squeezed the trigger.

The weapon fired, the muzzle flash stabbing into the darkness, pointed at the enemy soldier. The bullets hit him low in the back and lifted him. He sprawled forward, screaming.

"Fire!" Tynan yelled then. "Fire! Fire!"

He whirled then as the enemy began blasting the jungle around him. Bullets whipped through the air near him. They slammed into the trunk of the tree, stripping the bark. Bits of teak rained down. He dived to the left and rolled.

There was an explosion. A fountaining of orange fire. Shrapnel whirled through the night air. More men screamed. Firing rippled in the jungle. The area flashed and sparkled, looking as if all the photographers in the world were there with their flashbulbs.

"Coming at you!" yelled Jones.

Tynan saw two men breaking cover. He flipped the selector to full auto and squeezed the trigger. The flame reached out, almost touching the bodies of the Vietcong. Both of them fell as the bullets ripped into them.

"Over here," yelled Cummings.

"Got 'em," said Jones.

A Chicom grenade popped, sounding more like a big firecracker.

"Anyone hit?" demanded Tynan.

Firing tapered and then a single sustained burst came. The enemy, crouched at the base of a tree, was firing at the voice. Tracers glowing green flashed and bounced. There was a piercing scream as if the man was angry or terrified. He kept screaming, holding down the trigger.

Tynan aimed into the middle of the muzzle flashes and fired three times. The enemy's weapon fell silent, but the man continued to scream, his voice rising like a siren. A moment later he began shooting again. But the muzzle flashes were directed toward the jungle floor. The tracers slammed into the damp carpet of rotting vegetation. The voice became weaker as the weapon stopped firing.

"Let's go," yelled Tynan.

He slipped to the rear, away from the ambush site. He stopped, and waited. A instant later both Jones and Cummings appeared. When he saw them, Tynan turned, heading to the east. But he didn't run, he moved slowly, carefully, listening to the jungle behind him.

The only unnatural sound was the quiet moaning of a man hit in the ambush. He was crying softly and repeating the same word over and over again.

Tynan didn't care if the man was still alive nor did he care if any of the Vietcong who had been chasing them were still alive. The ambush had been designed to slow down the pursuit. That it had done.

They moved a hundred meters away and stopped for a moment. Tynan leaned against the trunk of a tree, staring into the jungle behind him. There was nothing to see except the charcoals and blacks of the night. There was a quiet rustling of the leaves overhead as an animal ran from one tree to another. A nightbird called softly, quietly. There was no sign of any pursuit.

"Let's get moving," said Tynan. "Jones, you're rear guard. You hear anything, let me know."

"Aye aye, Skipper."

Tynan plunged forward into the jungle, moving to the east. They crossed a shallow swampy area where the water came up to their knees. Not cool, refreshing water, but warm water filled with dirt and shit. The area smelled as if someone had emptied a septic tank into it.

They reached the other side and stopped for a moment. Tynan was afraid of leeches, but wasn't sure if they could survive in the polluted water. Besides, there was nothing they could do about them until they could see them.

They continued on, climbing a slight hill. There were sharp outcroppings of rock that glowed gray in the blackness of the night. They scrambled over them, reached the top of the hill, and looked out into the flatness of South Vietnam. The ground and jungle dropped away, giving him a view that could have reached the South China Sea, if it hadn't been night and if the air was clear enough.

To the north, near the place where Nui Ba Den would dominate the landscape and the huge American camp at Tay Ninh would be, there were flares in the sky. Bright points of green-yellow light that marked the base as clearly as spotlights and fences. Artillery crashed in the distance and there was an air strike going in to the east.

"Home," mumbled Jones as he stepped close to Tynan.

"Hardly," said the lieutenant. He looked at his

watch, the dial glowing in the dark. "Three hours of darkness left."

Cummings came up then. "There may be someone following us again."

Tynan crouched then and turned to the rear. "You sure of that?"

"No sir. Just heard a little noise back there."

"If the enemy had another patrol out," Jones said, "they might have picked us up after the ambush."

Tynan rubbed his sweat-damp face. He could feel the stubble of his beard, mixed with the dirt from the tunnels and the grit of days in the jungle.

"I think we'll just forget about them. Catch the others. If we've a problem, we can call in artillery. Let the cannon cockers take care of the situation for us."

"Aye aye," said Cummings.

"Let's move," Tynan said. He reached down, put a hand on a warm rock, and started the descent. The gentle slope was filled with fissures and pockmarked with craters. Somebody had shelled that side of the hill with something larger than hand grenades and 60mm mortars.

As they reached level land, the jungle thinned. Tynan took out the URC-10, extended the antenna, and heard the carried wave. He put the speaker to his ear and broke squelch three times. There was no response.

Undisturbed, Tynan continued to move to the east, watching the jungle around him as it thinned to little more than a light forest. Palm and coconut trees with a thin undergrowth. He veered to the right and then crouched under the branches of a flowering bush that smelled as if a perfume factory had exploded nearby. Again he broke squelch. This time he was rewarded by two clicks in response. Jacobs and the others were near him.

He stopped again, searching the landscape around him. He moved to the north and stopped. He had reached the edge of the jungle. It opened up into an expanse of rice paddies and a network of dikes. He glanced to the right and left, but Jacobs and his men were well hidden.

Jones joined him and said, "I'm sure we've got company."

Tynan touched the volume control of the URC-10, turning it down so that it would be barely audible. He keyed the mike and whispered, "Where are you?"

There was a four-second pause and then another voice said, "Edge of jungle. Come north."

Tynan wasn't sure how Jacobs knew he should come to the north, unless he'd moved that way himself.

"Roger."

As he reached up to collapse the antenna, a new voice erupted from the radio. "Your signal is weak. Do you need assistance?"

Ignoring that call, Tynan leaned close to Jones. "We move north. You and then Cummings. Pass the word."

Jones slipped off and then reappeared. When he was back, Tynan began to work his way to the north, at the edge of the jungle. Out through the trees, he could see the darkened landscape. There was a grove of trees about a hundred meters away, and in it he could see the black shape of a farmer's hootch. A water buffalo bellowed in the night. There was no light near the hootch.

They continued north for a hundred meters and then Tynan stopped. He listened to the sounds around him and surveyed the blackness of the jungle. There was nothing to hear or see. He stood up to take a step, and caught movement in front of him. Rather than challenge it, he slipped back to the ground.

"Come on in," said the voice. Tynan recognized it as Jacobs speaking.

Tynan stood again and said, "Coming in."

He met Jacobs at the edge of his tiny perimeter. He touched the big man on the shoulder. "Stopped one patrol but we think we've picked up another."

"How far behind?"

"Five, ten minutes."

"You think they'll want a fight?"

Tynan shook his head and knew that Jacobs wouldn't see the gesture in the dark. "No. I think they're going to wait to see what we do. Maybe hit the helos that come in to pick us up."

"We have choppers coming?"

"Just as soon as I get on the horn and call for them. Daybreak."

"Great," said Jacobs, his voice suddenly stronger. "I thought we were going to have to walk out."

Cummings moved closer and said, "The enemy patrol has stopped. I make it no more than twelve men."

"Shit," whispered Jacobs, "let's take them. We should be able to eliminate them before morning. Give us something to do to pass the time."

"You know," said Tynan, "I like the way you think."

Twenty minutes later, he'd briefed the men. Fifty to a hundred meters south of their location, the enemy had set up a camp to wait for the helos. They would use the time until morning to infiltrate that camp and eliminate the enemy. Knives and garrotes would be used. No shooting. An hour before dawn, they were to exfiltrate and return to the camp here. Transport would then be arranged.

Tynan waited as his men crawled off into the darkness. He followed then, using all the skills he had learned in a dozen military schools and on at least that many missions. In South Vietnam, they had to worry about booby traps and land mines. He wanted to be careful that he didn't rustle bushes and snap twigs. He crept close to the suspected location of the enemy, then got down on his belly to crawl the rest of the way. There was no reason to take stupid chances.

Tynan was back in his element. He knew exactly what he was doing and how he was going to do it. He moved one hand, set it down among the small plants on the moist surface of the jungle floor. He moved a foot, bringing it up toward his body. He lifted himself and shifted his weight forward, lowering himself to begin the process all over again.

Each time he stopped, he scanned the jungle, looking out of the corner of his eyes. He searched for a human shape, something that didn't exist in nature. He searched for something that didn't belong. At the same time, he used his nose and his ears. Humans tended to fidget and humans tended to disguise themselves with artificial scents.

He was halfway through a move when a noise caught his attention. His ears seemed to move by themselves, trying to find the noise again. Slowly he turned his head and spotted the VC no more than five feet from him. Tynan froze, watching the man, trying to figure out where he was looking by studying the squatting shadow that was lost in the blackness of the surrounding jungle.

For several minutes the man didn't move. He was as immobile as a block of granite and Tynan began to wonder if the jungle was conspiring to fool him. And then the man moved ever so slightly. Just enough so that Tynan could see that he was facing to the east, away from Tynan.

Slowly he turned and then came up to his feet. He crouched, his fingertips on the ground, his knees up, nearly touching his chin. He held his knife in his right hand, the sharp edge of the blade turned back toward him. He stared at the back of the VC's head, waiting. Then, like a jaguar, he sprung at the enemy soldier, grabbing him under the chin and lifting. As he dragged the body back, his hand clamped over the mouth and nose, lifting to expose the throat, he struck with the knife. It sliced through the thin skin of the neck. Blood spurted from the wound, landing on the plants near them, sounding like rain in the forest.

The Vietcong kicked out once as he died. His body went tense, as if he were going to fight back, and then sagged. The man's final breath rattled in his throat and Tynan felt him exhale.

As the man died, Tynan rolled the body away, felt the ground around them for the man's weapon, and stole it. Satisfied that he had done all he could, he began the slow retreat to their old position. He moved with the same care, knowing that men had died because they had assumed they were safe when they were far from it.

It took an hour to return, but Tynan didn't care. He stopped short, looked around, and then advanced carefully. He moved around, found that Jones was back, and learned that the younger man had killed two enemy soldiers. If the force was as small as they suspected, there wouldn't be much left of it by the time the sun rose and the helos arrived.

Moments later Cummings crawled back. He moved close to Tynan, grinned broadly, and held up a pistol he had captured. "Got the officer."

During the next twenty minutes each of the others returned. They had eliminated seven of the enemy soldiers, and even if they hadn't killed all of them, they had given those still alive something to worry about. When the sun rose, they would discover that someone had sneaked into their lines, killed some of their fellows, and then sneaked away. It was the same kind of terror tactic that the VC used against the Americans guarding base camp bunkers.

Tynan kept an eye on his watch and as dawn approached, he began trying to arrange for an airlift from their location. At first, he was unable to raise any of the airlift units in the area, but as it got later in the day, and the ground began to brighten, he found one unit that had been alerted to the possibility of having to extract his team. He gave them the proper recognition codes and was told that extraction would take place in one hour.

With the extraction arranged, Tynan leaned back and relaxed for the first time since they had entered the field. Now all he had to do was wait for the Army to pluck him and the team from the field.

With the sun high, shining down into the fist of jungle where they waited, Tynan surveyed the open fields around him. A farmer's hootch, invisible at night because it was built low on the corner of several rice paddies, stood a hundred yards away. The clump of trees he had seen earlier hid not one, but three, hootches. When the sun had risen, people had left the hootches—women to begin cooking the morning meal and men to begin their morning chores.

Tynan watched everyone carefully, but there was no sign that any of them were other than farmers and their families. No one seemed to be hostile.

Then, in the distance came the drumming beat of helicopter rotors. Tynan saw sunlight flash from the fuselages of the helicopters. He picked up the radio and told them he was there and waiting.

"Can you throw smoke?"

"Roger. Can throw smoke. Say when you want it."

"Wait one."

Tynan turned to his team and said, "Let's get ready. They'll land close to the trees. We'll want to be on the helos before they can touch down, if possible."

The men moved forward and crouched at the very edge of the jungle.

"Throw smoke" came the order over the radio.

Tynan set the radio down, pulled the pin on the grenade and threw it as far as he could. It hit a dike, bounced, and fell into the filthy water of the paddy. A moment later it began to billow purple.

"ID purple."

"Roger purple."

"Is the LZ cold?"

"LZ is currently cold but there are VC in the area. You may take some fire."

"Say location of the enemy."

"Just inside the trees, one hundred to two hundred meters south of the purple smoke."

"Roger. Guns will make a pass first."

Two helicopters broke away from the others, flew straight at the smoke, and then turned toward the south. A moment later, there were puffs of smoke behind the lead ship as it fired rockets into the trees.

The door gunners began to shoot, putting M60 rounds into the jungle.

As the lead ship broke away to the east, there was more firing, but this came from the jungle. Green tracers climbed into the sky but didn't hit the helo. The second ship turned slightly as if it was going to use the tracers as an aiming point.

The radio crackled to life. "Taking fire. AK and light machine guns."

"Inbound," said the pilot of the lead.

"Ready," said Tynan.

Two slicks suddenly dropped as if they had been raked by enemy fire. They dived at the purple smoke grenade, roaring out of the sky. In front of them, the gunships continued to rake the jungle with rocket and machine gun. As they broke around, the lead slick flared suddenly, the nose coming up and pointing nearly straight up so that Tynan could see the bottom of the ship.

As it slowed abruptly, the engine screaming and the rotors popping like a string of giant firecrackers, the skids leveled. The ship settled to the ground, the rotor wash fanning out, pushing at the water in the rice paddies.

Without a word to the others, Tynan ran from the jungle. He splashed through the knee-deep water of the rice paddy, his head bowed. There was a smile on his face because he knew he had just been saved several days of walking. Behind him he heard the shooting as the gunships worked to suppress the enemy. He reached the helo, put one foot up on the skid, and then reached up into the cargo compartment.

A hand grabbed him and hauled him in. He stumbled, a muddy foot slipping on the smooth gray of the deck. As he sprawled onto the troop seat, he turned and saw Jones climbing on board. The man was grinning broadly. And then the others were climbing in and the chopper was lifting off. It turned its tail to the jungle and the trees, racing across the open ground. When it neared the farmer's hootch, the pilot hauled back on the cyclic and the aircraft began a rapid climb.

Beside him, Jones screamed with pleasure. He was slapping himself on the legs and saying over and over, "We fucking did it! We fucking did it!"

Tynan glanced out as the ground fell away and he realized that the only danger left was the helicopter falling out of the sky. Not something to worry about. The Army pilots were as well trained in their jobs as Tynan and his boys were trained at theirs. The helicopter wasn't going to crash. They were as good as back at Nha Be.

And that meant that Jones was right: they had done it. Sneaked into Charlie's kitchen, raided his refrigerator, and then run off into the night. Charlie had chased them but he hadn't caught them.

Jacobs, sitting on the deck of the cargo compartment, turned and looked up at Tynan. His face was mud-spattered. The camouflage paint put on days earlier had run with the sweat, changing the pattern into something that was almost psychedelic, the black, green, and gray combining. He looked less than human, but he was happy. He wiped a hand over his face, rubbing at his forehead, smearing the camo grease even more. He held up his hand and laughed.

Tynan leaned against the transmission, listening to the roar of the engine. He wanted to sleep then, the strain of the last few days catching up with him all at once.

Jacobs slipped forward, touched Tynan's knee,

and, when he had the lieutenant's attention, asked, "What the hell you going to tell Walker about the COSVN?"

Tynan shook his head. "I'll think of something," he yelled back. "I'll think of something." But he wasn't sure that he would or that he cared. It was enough just to get in and to get out. Nothing else mattered.

He closed his eyes and let the sleep wash over him.

14

Tynan sat in Walker's office, letting the cool air from the ceiling fan and the air conditioner wash over him. He'd been at Nha Be only long enough to catch a shower, shave, and change into clean fatigues. But the shower had refreshed him and he planned on eating a big lunch before trying to sleep away the afternoon, evening, and night.

Walker sat behind his desk, his face buried in a report that was so important that he couldn't put it down long enough to acknowledge that Tynan was there. He read to the end of it, made a notation in the folder, and then carefully set it to one side. As he clasped his hands together, he glanced at Tynan and asked, "What do you have for me?"

"I'm back from my mission to the west," said Tynan.

"Obviously, and a little early," said Walker.

"Well, we ran into some problems, but did free an

American who had been captured a couple of days earlier."

"Yes," said Walker, waiting.

Tynan shrugged. "We made a preliminary recon of the area, but didn't find any evidence of a major headquarters—"

"It's there. You just have to look."

Tynan ignored the interruption. "Found evidence that the enemy, both Vietcong and the North Vietnamese, are using Cambodia as staging areas for their raids into South Vietnam. We found many camps and saw thousands of troops. Well, not actually saw them, but saw indications of them."

"The Communist headquarters," Walker said.

"None of the camps was well concealed. They were easy to spot. I think that's because the enemy doesn't expect us in Cambodia. We've made such a big deal out of the neutrality of the Cambodians that no one thinks we'll violate it. Charlie just wanders around as if he owns the place—which, I guess, he does."

Walker scratched his head and said, "Lieutenant, you were given a specific mission. Did you complete it?"

Tynan ignored the question. "Found evidence that the enemy was holding an American prisoner and managed to free him. I didn't get a chance to debrief him, but I imagine he'll have a lot to say to the intelligence boys."

"You're dodging the question, Lieutenant. Did you or did you not complete your mission?"

Tynan glanced at the floor and then looked up at Walker. "I would have to say yes and no to that."

Walker slapped the desk with his hand and yelled, "What in the hell does that mean?"

"It means," said Tynan, "that I didn't find the COSVN, but it's only because I don't think one exists. I think it's a myth invented by the brass hats in Saigon."

Walker's face, which had turned red with anger, now drained of its color. "You want to explain that?"

"It simply means that I don't think there is a major headquarters like the one we have in Saigon. I think there is one man who might coordinate the activity for the enemy in South Vietnam, but I don't think there is a staff, and therefore, I don't think there is a headquarters to do it. There is no COSVN as such. One man with the job, but no real bureaucratic structure that we can find and eliminate."

"Wrong," said Walker. "That is not acceptable."

"May not be acceptable," said Tynan, "but I believe that is the way it is."

"Then do you know who this man is?"

Tynan shook his head. "If I had to make a guess, I'd say Giap, but only because he engineered the French defeat at Dien Bien Phu. There was nothing that I saw that would suggest that he is the COSVN."

Walker stood up and moved to the window so that he could look out on the base at Nha Be. To the window he said, "Your guess is not adequate."

"Adequate or not, that is the only answer I have. Hell, we could roam about out there for months and not come up with anything else."

Walker returned to his desk and sat down. For a moment he didn't say anything. He stared down at the green felt blotter and the pen that lay on it.

"We had the chance to do something here to shorten the war," he said.

"Not if there's nothing to the information," said

Tynan. "If the COSVN doesn't exist, then we can't find it."

Resigning himself to the fact that the COSVN didn't exist in a form that could be exploited, or at least to the fact Tynan wouldn't admit it did, Walker said, "I'll expect a full, written report in the next two days."

Tynan stood up and said, "Anything about the prisoner we freed?"

"He's an Army man and he's their problem."

Tynan wanted to ask a couple other questions, but decided it wasn't the right time. He'd wait a couple of days. When Walker dismissed him, Tynan saluted and got the hell out. He figured that Jones or Jacobs would have the beers on ice and waiting. He hurried from the headquarters building.

Army Sergeant David Sinclair strolled into the company area with Boyson right behind him. He stopped, looked at the men sitting around in various stages of undress working on their equipment.

For a moment, no one looked up or said a word. Sinclair stood there watching and then asked, "Who wants to buy me a beer?"

"Buy your own," snapped one of the men.

Then another of them looked up and said, "Jesus H. Christ! Where in the fuck did you come from?"

With that the tent burst into cheering and shouting. The men leaped to their feet, surrounding Sinclair, slapping him on the back, and trying to shake his hand. They were shouting questions at him but not giving him a chance to answer. One man tried to press a Coke into his hand and another had a beer. They were laughing and screaming.

Sinclair raised his hands and laughed. "One at a time. One at a time."

"What in the hell happened?" shouted a man.

Sinclair turned and looked at Boyson. He pointed at the lieutenant. "You boys should thank the lieutenant. He's the one who came and got me."

"After leaving you to die in the jungle."

That silenced the group for a moment. Sinclair searched their faces and knew that he held the lieutenant's fate in his hands. The wrong word and the man would be unable to command. The right words and these men would follow him to hell if he asked them.

Sinclair also knew that he had a responsibility to those men. They had served in combat together. They had fought together and they had saved one another, and they would die together, if it came to that.

After a moment, Sinclair said, "The lieutenant came and got me. He got you men out rather than sacrificing you, and then came and got me."

"Shit," said someone.

And then another turned to Boyson and said, "Way to go, sir! Way to go."

Cheering erupted again as the men surrounded Boyson, trying to shake his hand.

Sinclair slipped out of the group and stood at the edge, watching. He sipped the beer he'd been handed and thought, *I did the right thing*. He felt better than he had since he'd walked into the jungle ambush what seemed to be a lifetime earlier. Much better.

THE WORLD'S MOST RUTHLESS
FIGHTING UNIT,
TAKING THE ART OF WARFARE
TO THE LIMIT — AND BEYOND!

SEALS #1: AMBUSH!   75189-5/$2.95US/$3.95Can
SEALS #2: BLACKBIRD   75190-9/$2.50US/$3.50Can
SEALS #3: RESCUE!   75191-7/$2.50US/$3.50Can
SEALS #4: TARGET!   75193-3/$2.95US/$3.95Can
SEALS #5: BREAKOUT!   75194-1/$2.95US/$3.95Can
SEALS #6: DESERT RAID   75195-X/$2.95US/$3.95Can
SEALS #7: RECON   75529-7/$2.95US/$3.95Can
SEALS #8: INFILTRATE!   75530-0/$2.95US/$3.95Can
SEALS #9: ASSAULT!   75532-7/$2.95US/$3.95Can
SEALS #10: SNIPER   75533-5/$2.95US/$3.95Can
SEALS #11: ATTACK!   75582-3/$2.95US/$3.95Can
SEALS #12: STRONGHOLD 75583-1/$2.95US/$3.95Can

and coming soon from Avon Books

SEALS #13: CRISIS!   75771-0/$2.95US/$3.50Can

CLASSIC ADVENTURES FROM THE DAYS OF THE OLD WEST FROM AMERICA'S AUTHENTIC STORYTELLERS

NORMAN A. FOX

DEAD END TRAIL	70298-3/$2.75US/$3.75Can
NIGHT PASSAGE	70295-9/$2.75US/$3.75Can
RECKONING AT RIMBOW	70297-5/$2.75US/$3.75Can
TALL MAN RIDING	70294-0/$2.75US/$3.75Can
STRANGER FROM ARIZONA	70296-7/$2.75US/$3.75Can
THE TREMBLING HILLS	70299-1/$2.75US/$3.75 Can

LAURAN PAINE

SKYE	70186-3/$2.75US/$3.75Can
THE MARSHAL	70187-1/$2.50US/$3.50Can
THE HOMESTEADERS	70185-5/$2.75US/$3.75Can

T.V. OLSEN

BREAK THE YOUNG LAND	75290-5/$2.75US/$3.75Can
KENO	75292-1/$2.75US/$3.95Can
THE MAN FROM NOWHERE	75293-X/$2.75US/$3.75Can